The Teahouse At The Edge Of The World

by Solala Towler

Also by Solala Towler

A Gathering of Cranes
Bringing the Tao to the West

Tales From the Tao
Inspirational Teachings From the Great Taoist Masters

Returning To The Source
Guided Meditations From the Daoist Tradition

Cha Dao: The Way of Tea

Tea Mind Tea Heart

More Tales From The Dao

Dragon Boy

Coyote Zen

Chuang Tzu: The Inner Chapters

The Tao of Intimacy and Ecstasy
Realizing the Promise of Spiritual Union

Practicing the Tao Te Ching
81 Steps on the Way

The Spirit of Zen
Teaching Stories on the Way to Enlightenment

Free and Easy Wandering
The Daoist Path From Fragmentation to Wholeness.

© 2023 by Solala Towler

Published by The Abode of the Eternal Dao
1991 Garfield St.
Eugene, Or 97405
www.abodetao.com

All rights reserved. No part of this book may be used or reproduced in any manner without written permission from the author and publisher.
ISBN: 9798867961411

For all lovers of tea and magic everywhere.....

The Teahouse At The Edge Of The World

Contents

Introduction
Chapter 1............2   The Seeker
Chaper 2..............9   The Celestial Teahouse
Chapter 3.........20   Tasting Tea
Chapter 4.........28   Do You Believe in Magic?
Chapter 5.........34   The Banished Immortal
Chapter 6.........44   The Teahouse For Ghosts
Chapter 7.........49   The Boy With Stones For Eyes
Chapter 8.........55   The Floating Teahouse
Chapter 9.........63   The True Story Of Jack and Jill
Chapter 10.......70   The Teahouse At The Edge Of
                                     The World Sutra
Chapter 11.......76   Dreaming Of Tea
Chapter 12.......84   The Boy Who Swallowed The Moon
Chapter 13.......90   The Man Who Knew Too Much
Chapter 14......104   Robot Tea
Chapter 15......110   The Teahouse For Ghosts Part Two
Chapter 16......113   Happy Endings
Epilogue.........121

Introduction

No one knows how long The Teahouse At The Edge Of The World has been there, or where it came from. There are various theories of course, but none of them tell the true and complete story of The Teahouse At The Edge Of The World, though some have parts of the story correct. But no theory is one hundred percent correct, and so it remains a total mystery to everyone.

Some people say it came from "nowhere," and some people say it has just always been there, like the sun. This seems like the likeliest story.

What *is* known is that it is impossible to go directly to The Teahouse At The Edge Of The World. One must just "find" him or herself there. It is not listed on any maps and is certainly not in any guidebooks. Some people say it exists in some kind of subliminal zone, just outside the periphery of consciousness. I have also been told that it is only by a "spiritual journey" that one can arrive there.

Another very interesting thing about The Teahouse At The Edge Of The World is that it looks and feels different to the different people who "end up" there. To some people it is a tiny shack; to others it is a palace. And the tea servers one meets there also are very different. They can be anything from an old woman to a ravishing young one. Or they can also be more than one person.

As mentioned, one cannot go there on purpose or by following any sort of map or set of instructions, at least not in the literal sense. Everyone who seems to find themselves there feels like it is some kind of accident or perhaps even divine intervention.

The one thing that everyone shares is that they have some kind of healing. Whether it is from the tea itself or the water it is brewed from or the interaction of the tea servers and the "customer", or whether it is the environment itself, is unclear. But, as you will see in the following pages, each person's story, though different, ends up with a sense of healing, of wholeness, and of a sense of greater peace in their being.

And while each story is different, and some quite fantastical, it seems these stories are as real as history and as true as time.

And if you are moved to share these stories with another, try reading them aloud. They really come alive that way in a differnt way than just sitting on the page.

Chapter One

The Seeker

The seeker had been seeking for so long he was sick of seeking. He often wanted to just give up and go back to his humdrum life where, if he was not happy, he at least was not driven by the need to seek. He was seeking the usual things — peace of mind, enlightenment, etc.

He had sat by the feet of many illustrious spiritual teachers, had spent a fortune on various workshops and private sessions with these teachers, some of whom were authentic teachers, while others were charlatans or worse. He had danced for hours chanting the holy names of various gods and goddesses, spent countless hours in deep meditation, had conjured up complicated and colorful mandalas in his mind, had twisted his body into ever more difficult yoga positions, had done breathing exercises until he was dizzy, had spent one long night puking into a plastic bucket after eating ayahuasca, but none of it helped.

None of it helped because, deep down inside himself, he did not truly believe in any of the practices he practiced and the reason for that was because, deep down, way down underneath everything else, he did not truly believe that he *deserved* to be happy, healthy, and possibly even enlightened.

Of course, several of his counselors, psychiatrists and even good friends had pointed this out, but he had always dismissed the idea, thinking *of course* he deserved all the good things of life. After all, he was a good person. He did not seek unfair advantage over anyone else. He did not steal or lie or abuse anyone. He was not a racist (he was pretty sure), he was not a sexist (so he believed), he was not a stupid person (so he hoped). All in all, he was a pretty decent guy and *of course* he deserved to be happy, healthy and possibly enlightened.

Maybe it was bad karma, he told his counselors and friends and even his girlfriend. He had been such a despicable person in his last lifetime that now he was paying for it. His Tibetan Buddhist friend had agreed with him, though not as passionately has he would have hoped. His girlfriend had agreed with him, though not as enthusiastically as he would have liked. Maybe he was not paying for evil deeds in his last lifetime, she had pointed out. Maybe he was paying for the thoughts and feelings he was having right now, in this lifetime, in this moment. Of course, they had ended up having a big argument about it and had agreed to disagree, though they had broken up soon after, though mostly likely, she had broken up with him.

It finally got to the point when he had given up on the whole idea of becoming enlightened and decided to just live a humdrum life of being nothing special, though he still harbored thoughts of enlightenment now and again. But then his Zen Buddhist friend had told him that the search for enlightenment was exactly what got in the way of true enlightenment, so he had even given that up.

The more he thought about it the more he was sure that just living a life without too much suffering was the best that he could do. He stopped all his spiritual practices, fired his counselor, and stopped hanging out with any of his Buddhist friends. He decided that what he needed was a vacation, a vacation from his own mind, if that were possible.

So signed up for a trek in the mountains of Nepal. True, it was a long ways away from San Francisco, where he lived, and was a much more challenging bit of hiking than what he was used to, and even a bit more Buddhist than what he would have liked, but he had heard that the Nepalese people were some of the friendliest people on the planet and that the views were magnificent and so signed up with a travel agency one of his old Buddhist friends had once told him about.

It was a long, long journey and he felt more than a little jet lagged and bit life lagged at the beginning but all the Nepalese folks at the guest house were so friendly and so warm and so nice that he quickly began to feel much more at ease. Actually, he ended up feeling much more at ease here in the Nepali guesthouse than he usually did at his own home in that shining city by the sea. It's true that the food did not agree with him, and he spent a fair amount of time in the bathroom, but it was all worth it. Eventually he found that if he just stuck to the rice and not the lentils, he did much better.

Finally came the day for the first hike. They had given him a few days to acclimate to the altitude. At first, he was huffing and puffing just walking from one level of the guesthouse to the next but after a few days he felt ready to do some hiking. The air felt so fresh, the light itself seemed different than at home and at night the stars seemed so close he could have put out his hand and touched them.

Unfortunately, the hiking itself did not go so well. He had to stop so many times to catch his breath and for his legs to stop shaking that he soon fell behind the group. The guide was having an animated conversation with a pretty girl from Sweden and did not notice and he was left alone and bereft on the trail, which for him had become a trail of tears.

His legs were shaking, he was breathing in large gasps and the fact that he was now alone on a mountain in Nepal did not seem nearly as romantic as he had envisioned when he had read the colorful brochure.

He looked wildly around but could see no one. He thought he had better retrace his steps back to the guesthouse but somehow, he had lost all sense of direction. At one point he just sat on the ground, slumped in sadness, and cried for about 20 minutes.

Finally, after wiping away his somewhat frozen tears, he got up and picked one direction, where the trail seemed to at least be going downhill and began to clomp his way down to what he hoped was the friendly (and warm) guesthouse.

But alas, the guesthouse did not appear, and he seemed to be getting more and more lost and more and more helpless and hapless until, all at once, he saw the outline of building, a little higher up, and a bit off the trail, so he made for it. Hopefully, he thought to himself, there will be some friendly Nepalese people there.

The closer he got to the little building the more ramshackle it appeared, so ramshackle that it looked as though one good wind or a large breeze would topple the whole thing over, whereupon it would undoubtedly roll all the way down the mountain.

Nevertheless, he pressed on and at last found himself at the door, which he banged on quite enthusiastically though no one answered his frantic pounding. After a while of fruitless knocking, he tried the door and found it unlocked. So, with a bit of trepidation, he opened it and looked into the gloomy, half dark room. There did not seemed to be anything in it but one small, very low table with two cushions, one on either side of the table.

He entered the room and looked around. There did not seem to be anyone there. He was so exhausted by this time that found himself sinking down onto one of the cushions. Presently, a very old woman appeared. Her back was so bent, with age or disease, that her head was at a perpendicular level to the floor, and she had to turn her head off to one side to look up at him.

"Well, hello there," she said, in Nepali but for some reason he could understand her as if she were speaking English. "You are just in time for tea." So saying, she hobbled over to the other side of the room and lifted a large metal kettle, which had been quietly bubbling over a small charcoal fire. It was quite a large kettle and looked very heavy, yet she lifted it with ease and practically skipped over to the table where he sat, feeling like he was in a dream.

This is a dream, he thought to himself. I have collapsed on the trail and am dreaming. Soon I will wake up unless I actually freeze to death on the mountain, which seemed a very likely possibility.

But no, he was not dreaming. As a matter of fact (or fancy) he was at The Teahouse At The Edge of the World, which of course he had never heard of. He sat and watched the old woman put the kettle down on the table, which almost toppled over, it was so heavy. She laughed a small and ancient laugh and adjusted the kettle so that the table righted itself again. Then she reached behind herself and produced a small clay teapot, a small clay bowl and two tiny cups.

The bowl held same dry and shriveled leaves and the old woman picked a small handful and placed them into the small clay teapot. Then, giggling like a schoolgirl, she poured hot water from the immense kettle into the pot and after just a moment or so, poured the golden liquid into the two tiny cups. She slid one over to her mystified guest and nodded at him expectantly.

Good heavens, he thought to himself, she wants me to drink this stuff, even though I have no idea what it is. What if she is trying to poison me? But she looked over at him with such a warm (and toothless) smile that he felt a bit reassured and dared to bring the tiny cup to his lips. It was very hot and he almost dropped it but managed to get a small sip and immediately felt better. He dared another sip and then another. The brew felt like warm gold running down his throat and into this belly. He felt himself smiling back at the old woman and even holding his cup out for more.

She filled his cup once again and once again he drank and felt the hot liquid move through his whole body. He felt like a warm hand was gently massaging his organs, from the inside of his body. What it is this stuff, he wondered? And, am I dying? But it felt so good that he decided that if he were dying, he didn't care.

For what seemed like a long time, he sat there, smiling back at the old woman, whose face seemed to shift from an old woman to a very young woman back to an old woman back to the young one again. He sat watching this like it was a movie unfurling before him. It didn't seem to frighten him, though later he wondered why.

He felt his lids growing heavy and he did not notice when he fell completely backwards onto the floor. He did not know how long he was out but when he came to the old woman was gone and he was alone in the rickety building, which seemed to be swaying slightly in the breeze. He stumbled out the door and by some kind of miracle, found the right trail back to the guesthouse, though he had no idea how, and found his own room and collapsed onto his bed, with its thin mattress and warm blanket and slept some more.

In the middle of the night, he got up to pee and stepped outside for a moment, gazing up at the close, close stars and wondered what had just happened to him and why did he feel so good and so peaceful? It felt as though all the worrying and searching that he had been doing in the last few years as a dedicated seeker seemed as though they had happened to someone else, not him. Not to the guy who was standing out under the glistening stars somewhere in the mountains at the edge of the world, here in far off Nepal. Except that it was not actually far off but right here and right now.

Of course, when he told his guide, who had been worried about him and sure that he was about to be fired, about the rickety building and the old woman and the magical tea, he just laughed at him and said it was probably the altitude playing tricks on his mind.

But he knew better, he felt better, and he decided not to argue with the guide and instead keep the whole experience to himself, as if it were a precious treasure, which it was. Though he often thought to himself, what the hell was in that tea anyway? But, in the end, as in the beginning, it didn't really matter what was in the tea. Magic, he thought, deep down in his being, magic tea.

He was a bit worried that once he got home and back to his normal routine that the glow of his experience at the Teahouse At The Edge of the World would fade but it did not. Instead, it seemed to grow and he felt more at peace with himself than he had ever in his life. He tried to tell a few of his friends about it but they looked at him as if it were a dream he was describing and not something that had actually happened to him. Even his Buddhist friends were a bit skeptical but when he told his ex-girlfriend about it, she began to look at him in a new light. He felt different, she said, more solid, less obscure, clearer, and more grounded and even, dare she say it, happy.

And the truth was that he *was* happy and more solid etc. He often lay back on his bed in the middle of the night, looking up at the ceiling and seeming to see the clear and bright Nepalese stars winking and glistening at him. And if he reached out his hand, even a little, he was able to gather them up and pour them into his heart, where they bubbled gently away like a teakettle made of light.

Chapter Two

The Celestial Teahouse

Zhu Hui was traveling to Xian, the capital of Tang, to take part in the national examinations. He had been studying for some years now, in hopes of passing with high marks, making him eligible for a high-level posting in the Tang government. This would not only make his fortune, but also elevate his entire family. Needless to say, the pressure to do well was definitely very high. Zhu Hui was already the nervous type, and he was feeling *very* nervous now.

His father had given him a small amount of money for his expenses and Zhu Hui had to be very careful, as it was not a large amount, and prices in the capital would undoubtedly be very high. So he was being very careful not to spend much of it along the way, only enough for a rough bed at an inexpensive inn, along with a bowl of rice.

But the one thing that Zhu Hui could not do without was tea. He actually had paid more for tea than for his rice in the inns along the way to the capital. He had been a deep lover of tea since his grandfather has introduced him to the Way of Tea when he was very young, too young to really understand what his grandfather had told him about Cha Dao. But as he grew up, he appreciated more and more the time he had spent with his grandfather before his death.

Not only had his grandfather introduced him to the Way of Tea but of high-quality tea. "It is useless to drink low quality tea," his grandfather had said. "You would not only be throwing your money away, but you would be introducing poison to your body. Only drink high quality tea and it will allow your qi to flourish and you will live to an old and healthy age, as I have."

It was true that his grandfather *had* lived a long and happy life. He had been very aged indeed but always had a smile on his face, especially when he sat in his small garden, sipping his beloved tea. He was a follower of the great tea master Lu Yu, who had written the definitive treatise on all things tea, his Cha Jing. In it he had listed all the best qualities, not only of tea and tea utensils but also of the water to be used.

Lu Yu had this to say about water for tea: "Water made from mountain streams is best, while river water is permissible if stream water is not available. Well water is to be avoided." The reason, according to Zhu Hui's grandfather, is that well water is stagnant and so has no qi; or the qi is not conducive to healthy tea. The tea must have enough qi of its own so that it can mix with the qi of the drinker and raise their spirits.

"Water from slow moving mountain streams is the best for good quality tea," said Lu Yu. "Stone-lined pools are also good. But, he warned, never take water that falls in cascades, gushes from a spring, rushes in a torrent. The qi in this kind of water will lead to illness of the throat."

Zhu Hui's grandfather had shared the famous story of when the tea master went to visit a local dignitary when he was on a visit to his favorite river, the *Wusongjian*, in Suzhou province. The nervous dignitary, who wanted to impress the famous tea master, told his servant to take a boat out on the river to gather water from precisely the middle of the river, where the current flowed slow and strong. But, on coming back to shore, the boat knocked against the dock and some of the precious mid-river water spilled out. Afraid that he was going to be late, the servant hurriedly scooped some water by the side of the bank, sure his master would not know the difference.

Unfortunately, upon tasting the tea, Lu Yu said, "This tea is very good quality but the water it was steeped in is a bit inferior."

"Oh no," said the nervous dignitary. "I had it especially taken from the very middle of the freely flowing river."

At this the very frightened servant confessed about spilling the water and adding the inferior water from the bank. The dignitary was very embarrassed and angry and wanted to punish the servant severely, but Lu Yu stopped him, saying it was not really the fault of the servant but the fault of the boat, which had bumped the dock and spilled the water.

It had seemed to Zhu Hui, when his grandfather had told him this story, that it was a bit far-fetched, but his grandfather had insisted that true tea masters could tell not only where the tea leaves came from in any given tea, but where the water was from as well!

How Zhu Hui had loved sitting with his grandfather and drinking good tea, under the shade of the osmanthus tree in the far back courtyard where his grandfather had lived. His grandfather had been so proud when Zhu Hui had told him that he had been accepted as a scholar and had been given permission to sit for the national examinations in the capitol.

Of course, Zhu Hui needed to spend most of his time studying after that and did not have the time to spend sitting under the ancient osmanthus tree, drinking tea with his grandfather, and listening to his tales of tea. And while his grandfather was very sad about this, he was also very proud and excited about his grandson becoming a scholar, the highest rank in Chinese society, and so did not complain when their teatime was severely curtailed.

Now Zhu Hui was almost at the capital, where the exam would be held. The exam itself lasted for three days and the students were locked into minuscule rooms, with nothing but a few planks of raw wood, which served as table, bench, and bed. They would be stuck there, going through the examination books, and writing in careful calligraphy. They were graded, not only on their answers to the questions in the book, but also on their penmanship, which was equally important as their answers. Many students, who had labored so laboriously over their papers, upon being extremely tired by the end, had botched a few characters and had been failed because of that, no matter how well they knew the material.

Out of the three thousand students who took the examination, only a handful passed, at least on their first attempt. Many of them tried several times to pass, as they were allowed to retake the test if they wished. On the other hand, there were many tales of disappointed and distraught young scholars who took their own lives rather than to return to their villages and homes in disgrace.

The whole thing would make anyone highly nervous about their fate, and as Zhu Hui was already the nervous type, it seems rather hopeless to him that he would succeed where so many other, equally talented scholars, had failed. But his beloved grandfather's last words to him were about how proud his was that his grandson would be raising the whole family when he returned from the capitol, garlanded in glory. So even though he really would have been happier to just live a simple life of a clerk or a village teacher, Zhu Hui had gathered himself and set off for the capitol and his fate, whatever that proved to be.

When his grandfather had died, Zui Hui did inherit some very good quality tea but it had all been drunk up in the endless nights that he had spent studying for the examination. His father had wanted to complain about how much lamp oil he was using up, but his mother intervened, telling his father that it would all be worth it when their young scholar son returned from the capitol, when he would surely be given a high position in the government. His whole family had been so proud, though his mother did notice the dark circles under his eyes and how he had seemed to develop a nervous tick in one of them.

But now, here he was, a full ten months later, and nearing his goal. He had almost reached the capitol but, thinking how expensive the inns were sure to be there, he decided to stop a little before the capitol and stay in a less expensive one on the outskirts of the great city.

He had walked all the way from his village to the capitol, being too poor to afford a carriage or even a cart, not to mention a horse. He had been passed many times on his journey by gaily waving young scholars who were being driven by family servants. He had even seen one slightly fat and obviously wealthy scholar, being born on the back of his servant! He too had waved gaily at Zhu Hui, while the servant huffed and puffed along the dusty road.

Presently he came to a homey looking and somewhat dilapidated teahouse. Because of its slightly run-down look, Zhu Hui figured it would be more affordable than one of higher quality. When he timidly knocked at the gate, it was immediately opened by an old woman, who smiled such a warm and inviting smile at him, that Zhu Hui felted happy and flattered to receive such a welcome. She bowed to him and even curtsied a little, and bade him enter, while still bestowing such a warm smile upon him that he felt himself blushing. The woman noticed and chuckled a little, then turned and led him into the teahouse itself.

Once inside the courtyard, Zhu Hui saw that it was much less run-down looking than from the outside. He worried for a moment if he would truly afford it, but the old woman gestured for him to enter the main building and he decided he could at least stop and have some tea. He felt sure that the tea here would be of good quality.

The two of them entered a large room, which was furnished with simple yet expensive looking furniture. It all looked like antiques to Zhu Hui. Not only that, but he noticed that the old woman was wearing a robe that looked more like paintings he had seen from the Han Dynasty, more than 500 years before Tang. They didn't look old either, but as if they had been made recently. Perhaps, he thought to himself, this old woman likes the fashions of that long ago time and makes her clothing to look like Han.

The old woman bade him sit at one of the low tables in the very middle of the room. Zhu Hui did not see anyone else in the room, which seemed a bit odd, since this teahouse was so close to the capitol. Perhaps it was the early hour, he thought to himself.

He decided to speak right up and let his hostess know that he was not one of the wealthy scholars on his way to take the examination but one of the very poor ones. But she just smiled and said, "That is all right, young lord. We serve all levels of society here."

Zhu Hui tried to tell her he was no "young lord," but she turned away just as he began to speak. "I will bring you something hot to eat and perhaps some tea?" she ended in a kind of question.

Zhu Hui's spirit picked up. He was sure that this elegant woman would know what kind of tea to serve such a one as he. "I cannot afford anything too dear," he began, but she had already left the room. He sat there for a while, marveling at all the many sumptuous scroll paintings that lined the walls of the room. Some of them looked much like the ones he had seen in books, that had been painted by ancient masters, but he figured they were just copies of the originals, something that was common in China in that time. There was just no way that they could be originals, he thought to himself.

He had just gotten up from his table to take a closer look at some of them, when the woman came back with a large bowl of soup, which smelled of ginger and other aromatic spices. She laid it down on the table, which already had an empty bowl and a soup spoon, along with chopsticks. The soup had a fragrance that seemed otherworldly to him. He had never smelled such a delicious soup and before he knew it, he was gobbling it down, as if he had not eaten in days.

Just when he thought he could eat no more, the old woman came out with a tea pot and two small teabowls. (In the days of Tang people drank tea out of small bowls rather than cups.) Well, he thought to himself, there is always room for tea!

He saw the two cups and assumed the old woman would be drinking tea with him, but as soon as she laid the pot and cups on the table she bowed to Zhu Hui and left the room. Alone, he lifted the cover of the teapot and gave the contents a sniff. The aroma of the tea wafted into his nostrils and went straight to his heart, bypassing his head altogether. He felt on the edge of passing out, it was so good. It seemed to fill his whole body with a wonderful feeling of lightness and buoyancy.

He was almost afraid to taste it, fearing it would send him into a state of unconscious bliss, but just as he lift the pot to pour the tea, another woman suddenly entered the room.

This woman was much younger and so beautiful he again felt himself on the edge of passing out, he was so struck with her beauty and poise. She bowed very prettily to him and introduced herself as Peony. Zhu Hui wondered for a moment if she was a "flower girl" or prostitute, but her manner was so delicate that he soon realized he was probably in the presence of a highly refined woman. Perhaps she was of some aristocratic family that had seen hard times and so she had to work in this undistinguished teahouse.

Peony took the teapot from his hands and began to pour the tea into the two small bowls. Zhu Hui sat, transfixed, both at her beauty and the way she held the teapot in her small and delicate hand, as if she were holding a flower. The tea itself smelled of flowers and earth and other exotic flavors. It was not a tea that he was at all familiar with, though he had drunk and even studied many kinds of tea.

Peony laid the teapot back down on the table with a graceful movement of her hand, as if she were dancing. All of her movements were so full of grace and balance and beauty. Zhu Hui had never seen anything like it. She smiled at him, a small but warm smile and slid one of the teabowls over to him. She noticed that he was still staring at her stupidly and said in a small and surprisingly low voice. "Drink, Young Master, before the tea gets cold."

Zhu Hui came to with a start, and Peony laughed a little, hiding her mouth behind the large sleeve of her robe. He noticed then that she also seemed to be wearing the clothing of the Han. The people of this inn, he thought to himself, seem to be entranced with the fashions of that olden age, considered by many scholars as the first golden age of the Middle Kingdom. Now, of course, it was the Glorious Tang, and society, politics and the arts were at the highest culmination in all of history.

Zhu Hui tore his gaze from his companion and addressed the tea, as his grandfather had taught him how to do. First he looked at the color of the tea, which connected the tea with his eyes, which opened to his *shen*, or spiritual heart. Then he smelled the tea, once again marveling at its fragrance, which connected to his qi or vital energy body. Then he sipped it slowly, taking three small sips and tasting each with a different part of his tongue. In this way, each part of his tongue woke up in different stages.

Not surprisingly, the tea was excellent. Actually, it was *more* than excellent. He felt himself being carried off on waves of delight. It was simply the best tea he had ever tasted. Along with its exquisite taste it also had a wonderful feeling of deep *qi* and he felt it penetrating his whole body, all the way down to the deepest part of him.

Once he had emptied his cup, Peony immediately filled it again. Zhu Hui was not used to be treated in such an elegant manner, by someone so elegant herself. As a matter of fact, he had never even *met* someone so elegant and beautiful. He had to remind himself that he was just a poor scholar and of course could never hope to unite himself with a woman as elegant and beautiful as Peony. But he did enjoy being waited upon by her, here in this surprisingly elegant and interesting place, surrounded, as it was, by so many ancient and beautiful paintings of so long ago.

The other surprising thing was that each cup of tea tasted better than the last one. He was used to drinking tea, even the best tea that he had inherited from his grandfather and finding that with each steeping the tea lost something of flavor and qi, but this tea kept getting even more flavorful and full of qi with each steeping. He had to stop himself a few times from just emptying each bowl with one gulp and instead drink it very slowly, savoring each sip. This was what his grandfather had called *pin ming*, savoring tea, rather than just drinking it down, like a common laborer.

Peony went over to the side of the room and picked up a *guqin*, an ancient seven stringed instrument, beloved by all scholars and sages in China. "May I play something for you, Young Master," she asked.

Of course, Zhu Hui could not say no, and he assented vigorously. Peony began playing, at first very slowly, then a little faster, though never too fast. It was important to create and sustain a certain mood of tranquility and peace with the music.

Zhu Hui sat there, entranced by the music, the tea, and the beauty of of Peony's playing. He was reminded of an old story about the guqin. It had happened in the Spring and Autumn era, in the kingdom of Chu, long before the Tang. A renowned master of the guqin, named Boya. He was famous for his exquisite playing and performed for many high-ranking people but he most liked to play his instrument out in nature.

One day he had hiked into the mountains and spent the night in a little woodcutter's hut. He was all alone there under a spacious moon, and he played only for himself and the moon. Suddenly he broke a string, which was of such a momentous occasion that he was sure that his qi had been distracted because someone unknown had been listening to him playing. He opened the door of the hut and found a woodcutter standing there, entranced by the music, with tears streaming down his face.

Boya invited him in into the hut and, after replacing the broken string, played for his new friend, whose name was Zhong Ziqi. Ziqi told him that he had been drawn to the hut by the heavenly music that he had heard coming out of the usually quite silent hut. He described what he had heard as "lofty as a mountain" and as "the vast spirit of freely flowing water." Boya bowed to his new friend and said, "Your heart is the same as mine." They spent the rest of the night conversing and laughing as Boya played tune after tune on his beloved instrument.

Boya always visited with Ziqi whenever he was in the mountains, and they spent many hours of joyful sharing. Then, on one of his trips to the mountains he learned that Ziqin had died. Boya went to his friend's tomb and played for him one last time and then smashed his beloved instrument in pieces, saying, "Now that my friend has died, of what use is it for me to play the guqin?"

Zhu Hui had always been moved by this story. As a matter of fact, the characters, *zhi yin*, described someone who is moved by music. Later on, it came to mean "intimate friend," or "soul mate."

The time passed slowly as Zhu Hui sat, entranced by the tea, the music, and the presence of Peony. Suddenly, he felt very sleepy and felt himself drifting downward, as if he were sinking into a warm pool. He wanted to thank Peony and the old woman for all that they had done for him, but he found that he could not speak, he was so sleepy. He had a brief thought of asking if there was a bed he could lie on until he could regain his strength but even that was too much. He felt himself drifting down and down, his belly full of amazing tea and his heart full of beautiful music. Truly he felt as a zhi yin.

He did not know how long he had slept but when he awakened, he found himself lying on the ground. Astonished, he sat up quickly and looked around. He could see no sign of the teahouse. Perhaps they had dragged me out here to sleep on the earth, he thought, though he could see no reason why they would.

He picked himself up slowly and made his way to the capitol. Strangely though, he felt so lighthearted and spirited, his feet barely touched the ground he trod on, and his head was filled with the sweet perfume of the magical tea and his heart was filled with the magical presence of sweet Peony.

Once there, he asked around about the strange teahouse, where the women dressed in ancient clothing and served such exquisite tea, but no one seemed to know anything about it. So for a while, he forgot about it, as he needed to apply himself to the examinations. Amazingly, at least to him, he placed among the highest grade and was offered a place as an assistant to a magistrate in a prefecture near his hometown.

On the last night he was in the capitol, he had gone to a very elegant teahouse to celebrate with some of his new friends, all who had also placed highly in the examinations. He was enjoying drinking some very high-level tea that evening, although it was not as nearly high-level, as the tea Peony had served him, when suddenly he was drawn to a scroll painting that was hung in a place of high regard. He found himself walking over to the painting and looking at it very closely.

The style of painting was of a very old one, used mainly in the Han Dynasty, hundreds of years before the Tang. It was of a beautiful woman playing the guqin for a gentlemen scholar, who sat entranced before a bowl of tea. The closer he looked at it, the clearer it became that the beautiful woman was none other than Peony and that the gentleman scholar was none other than himself!

He managed to buy the painting, which though superb, was a copy of the original and so he was able to afford it by borrowing a little from his new friends. He carried it back to his hometown, and then to where he was stationed and hung it on the wall of his tearoom and spent many joyful hours staring at the beautiful painting and wondering how he had found himself in such a wonderful, mysterious, and even celestial teahouse.

Chapter Three

Tasting Tea

Mei Lin had been brought to Mei Guo (US) from her birth country of Zhong Guo (China) when she was a young girl. When she was around 12, her family went back to China for a visit. They had spent some sweltering weeks in Hangzhou, where her mother and father had met, and also where her grandfather and grandmother had met, not long after the nation-wide insanity of the Cultural Revolution had died down.

Mei Lin's grandmother had seemed like a ghostly presence. Her suffering during the long years of repression and cultural devastation was very deep and she never talked about it, even to her children, and certainly not to her grandchild.

Her grandfather also chose not to talk about those years, even though he had suffered even more than her grandmother. He was happy just to sit in his tiny tearoom at the back of their tiny apartment. He also liked to take long walks around the beautiful West Lake. He often took Mei Lin on his walks. He never spoke much at these times, but Mei Lin was one of those rare children who was comfortable with silence.

He even took her on a boat ride around the lake. It had been so peaceful out on the water, while the boatman silently rowed the boat. She and her grandfather had drunk fresh Dragon Well green tea and looked off into the distance where they could see a tall pagoda and the often-hazy outlines of the city.

Hangzhou had once been the capital city, during the Yuan Dynasty, when the fierce Mongols had ruled China. It was the city that Marco Polo, that legendary traveler from Italy, called one of the most beautiful cities in the world.

In ancient times people believed that it was indeed one of the most beautiful cities in China, along with Suzhou, noted for its many canals and traditional gardens. As a matter of fact, there was an old saying: "Heaven above, Hangzhou and Suzhou below."

One other thing that Mei Lin and her grandfather had done was sit in his tiny tearoom and drink old tea. Old tea, not in the sense of bad or moldy, but more in the sense of being aged, like a fine wine.

"This tea that we are about to drink," he would say, holding up a wooden container of well-aged *sheng puerh* tea, "has been on my shelf for 20 years. And before that it sat on another shelf at the teashop for another ten years. All this time it has been silently working to become the magical brew that we are now about to drink."

Mei Lin thought it was a little gross to drink tea that was 30 years old. She knew that the Lipton tea that her mother and father drank back home in the States was freshly bought at least once a week. Not only that, but her parent's tea did not look so darkly brown and smell like damp earth.

But she had held her tongue and her nose and drank the tea her grandfather, her Yeh Yeh, poured her, but she did not enjoy it. But she did enjoy spending time with him. She was fascinated by the tea preparation itself. Her grandfather would heat water to just the right temperature, until the water was bubbling with what tea masters called "fisheyes." The he would first pour the fish-eye water into a tiny teapot and into two tiny cups to heat them up. The teapot and cups were made of a special clay called *yixing* and had been used for tea utensils for hundreds of years.

Chapter Three

The tea came in a tightly pressed brick, which had to be broken up with a small knife. Then he would put a small amount of tea into the teapot. After a very short time he would pour the first steeping out into a bowl that sat on his tea table. "This first steeping," he would say," is just to wake the tea up. It has been sleeping in its brick form for over thirty years now and the leaves need to open and share with us their flavor and medicine."

Mei Lin had never heard anyone refer to tea as medicine. To her, medicine was some awful tasting thing that her mother forced her to drink when she was sick. And while the tea her grandfather shared with her tasted pretty weird, it was not as awful as the awful medicine her mother gave her.

Then, after pouring out the first steeping of the tea, he would pour more hot water into the teapot and then, almost immediately, pour it into another small vessel and from there into the tiny teacups. Each one of them could fit into Mei Lin's hand, even though her hands were pretty small.

Of course, there was not a lot of tea in each cup, barely one or two mouthfulls, but her grandfather somehow made it seem that it was a much larger cup than it was. He would often take several minutes to drink the tea, sipping it slowly and with great enjoyment. "Our ancestors have drunk tea in this way for thousands of years," he would say. "A professor friend of mine once told me that there are cave paintings three thousand years old of people making offerings to the ancient tea trees."

Mei Lin knew she was supposed to be impressed by this, but it just seemed a little weird to make offerings to an old tree. But she held her tongue and pretended to be impressed by these tidbits of history and nodded her head in a serious way. Her grandfather had smiled at her then, though she later realized that he had seen right through her. After all, she had been raised in Mei Guo, the Beautiful Country, which though it was undoubtedly beautiful, was a country of barbarians.

The Chinese country, Zhong Guo, the Middle Kingdom, had been the center of culture and wisdom for thousands of years and would undoubtedly be so for many more. True, in its long history it had many ups and downs, such as the not-so-long ago years of the Cultural Revolution, when people were told to destroy the "four old's": old things, old ideas, old customs and old habits.

Much of Chinese traditional culture had been destroyed in this so-called Cultural Revolution, but eventually things turned around and now many people knew the value of the traditional Chinese culture, though not many young people, it was true. It was mostly the old ones like himself that valued these things. Young people of today were just interested in making money. And if it were not for tourist money, what remained of much of the traditional culture of temples and historical landmarks would probably have been torn down long ago. Many foreigners, who in his youth, had been called *gwailou*, or foreign devils, were fascinated with the old temples and old stories of China.

Her grandfather, her Yeh Yeh, had seemed so happy there in his tiny tearoom, sipping the old tea from tiny teacups. Mei Lin knew that he was hoping to pass on the spirit of tea and of his own spirit with tea during these times, but she was too young, too American, already too much of a gwailou, to really appreciate it.

"Chinese people have always drunk tea," he told her. "It is a part of the Chinese culture, just like writing with graceful characters or pictures, instead of the ungainly scribbling of Westerners.

"It is when we drink tea, in a relaxed and unhurried fashion," he went on, "that we are truly in touch with our ancestors, those who have gone before us, past the Yellow Springs of death. In turn, we ourselves will become ancestors to our decedents, down through all of time.

"China has been here for a long, long time and will be here for many, many years to come. Our governments may come and go, whole dynasties may fall and rise, but the people of China will always go on.

"We say," he went on, "'*Dha de ziwei zhi renqing wei*', or 'the true flavor of tea is that of human affection'. Of course, many people just guzzle their tea all day long and never take the time to even taste what it is they are guzzling. But some of us know that to take the time for tea is like taking time for our own spirits, our heart, our own shen. It is when we slow down and really savor the tea, what we call *pin ming*, that the tea is able to taste us as we taste it."

He had died soon after and so Mei Lin never got to spend more time with him and tea. Later on, she wished she had asked him more questions about Cha Dao, the Way of Tea, when she had the chance. She wished she had asked him what happened to him and her grandmother, her Nai Nai, during the Cultural Revolution, but she hadn't and now it was too late. Her grandmother passed over the Yellow Springs of death soon after her grandfather had. So now she had no more ties to the Motherland, since her grandparents on the other side had died already long before.

Later, much later, after she had gone to college and graduated at the top of her class and had begun a career in chemistry, did she begin to think about that old tea and that magical time with her kindly grandfather. She decided that she would buy some of that *puerh* tea and see if she would taste a little of that magical time with her Yeh Yeh. So she went down to the local Chinatown, which was crowded with many little shops selling all kinds of Chinese clothing and tchokes and found a teashop with the strange name of The Teahouse At The Edge of the World.

She entered the shop and looked around at the many shelves of many kinds of tea. The room had a strange kind of herbal smell, a little sweet and a little bitter. Just like life, she thought to herself.

She wandered around the shop looking and even sniffing the different kinds of tea on display there. There seemed to be many shelves of large round cakes of tea that looked somewhat like the kind she had drunk with her grandfather.

After a little while, a young women came into the room and asked very pleasantly if she could be of service. Mei Lin had been charmed by her phrasing and also quite charmed with her voice, which was low and even a bit hoarse, yet sounded so sweet in her ears.

"I am looking for some puerh tea," she said, "like I once drank in China."

"*Mei wen ti*," said the woman, in Chinese, "no problem," and went behind the counter, where Mei Lin could see many round cakes of dried tea, some which had quite elaborate wrappings.

(It was a bit strange but even though Mei Lin did not actually speak Chinese, she understood exactly what the woman had said.)

She was not too sure what kind to buy. She had thought that there was only one kind, the one that she had drunk with her grandfather, but she learned that there were not only two main kinds or strains of puerh, but that the store carried a bewildering variety of them. The kind she had drunk with her grandfather, the old tea, was probably *sheng* or raw puerh, the owner of the tea shop told her. This was the naturally aged and fermented kind. The other, the cooked or *shou*, was "fast tracked" in order to take on some of the properties of the sheng. It was processed and then piled, wet down, and covered with a thermal blanket to keep the heat that was created in the piling in the tea itself so that it was fermented in a fraction of the time the original or sheng did.

When she asked about 30-year-old sheng the woman had laughed. "Oh," she had said, "I don't carry any kind of very expensive tea like that. It would cost a minimum of $3,000 a cake." She had very few customers who were interested in that kind of tea or could even afford it if they were.

One thing that Mei Lin liked about her is that her eyes were soft, just like her grandfather's. And when she put the tea into Mei Lin's hands, she put her own hand over Mei Lin's for a brief moment and they felt so warm and even kind, if such a thing were possible, which apparently, it was.

So she had bought a little of each kind and went home with a curious feeling of excitement and dread. She had also bought a small yixing teapot and two tiny cups, the kind of cups she had drunk from with her grandfather so long ago. This is just an experiment, she told herself.

After all she was a scientist and that is what scientists do, experiment.

When she got home, she put water in the teakettle and waited until she heard it bubbling, hopefully with "fisheye" bubbles. Then she poured a little into the teapot and then poured it out into a bowl. Then she put a small amount of tea into the pot and filled with water. She was not sure how long to let it steep, but she had started with the shou or cooked tea and was pretty sure she could let it steep for a few minutes.

When she poured out the first steeping it was pretty clear, and she was thinking she might have to put more leaves in but when she poured out the next steeping it was pretty dark and when she poured out a third steeping it was as dark as coffee.

She sat at her chair at her kitchen table and sipped the tea. She lived alone and so did not have to explain her "experiment" to anyone else. At first the tea tasted really strong, and she was not sure she liked it. It felt almost as if she were drinking a mud puddle! But she drank the next steeping and the next and it began to grow on her. The owner of the teashop and told her that with good quality tea, she could steep it a dozen times or more. But she wanted to taste the other one so she stopped after five steepings.

She cleaned out the teapot and added more hot water and some of the the other tea, the sheng, what she was already thinking of as her "grandfather tea." She remembered that her grandfather had steeped that very quickly, what the teashop owner had told her was "flash steeping." Any longer than that, she was told, would create a very bitter brew.

The Chinese have a phrase, she remembered, *chi ku*. It meant "eating bitter," or the ability to put up with a lot of suffering. She was sure that both of her grandparents had eaten plenty of bitter in their days as slaves on a farm out in western China, where they had been sent during the Cultural Revolution. Being intellectuals, they were viewed as class enemies and so were sentenced to hard labor on a farm. And of course, being intellectuals, they had never worked on a farm or even done much manual labor, and so suffered endlessly.

She tried a sip of the sheng. It was slightly bitter. Perhaps she had steeped it too long, she thought to herself. She tried another sip and was suddenly transported to that long ago afternoon in that long ago time in that long ago place. It was as if she were sitting with her grandfather, sipping tea, listening to him talk about the Chinese people and how they were so intimately connected to the Way of Tea.

So much of what he had said to her in that long ago time had gone completely over her young head. But now she began to understand a bit of what he had been trying to communicate to her. She who had grown up in Mei Guo, with her totally assimilated parents. She who had never felt particularly Chinese, not in the way her grandfather had felt, not in the way her way-back ancestors had felt. But now, sitting here and sipping this strange tea, she felt more Chinese than she had ever felt before. Oh how she wished her Yeh Yeh were still here so that she could ask him about this mysterious *Cha Dao*. She wanted so much to be able to drink some tiny cups of that aged and very fine tea, and to sit with him and listen to him talk about what it really meant to be Chinese.

But, in a way, she was able now, to taste the taste of the tea tasting her and remember, in her deepest heart, what it felt like to be in the presence of her grandfather and his Way of Tea, like a seed that he had planted in her so long ago and that had taken so long to come to fruition.

Later on, on another day, she had gone back to Chinatown to visit that strange teashop called The Teahouse At The End of The World, but it was gone and no one in the neighborhood had any idea of where it had moved to. She found another teashop and bought some precious sheng puerh tea, but it did not taste the same in the magical way as the tea that she had gotten at The Teahouse At The End of The World. But it would have to do, she thought to herself, and it did.

Chapter Four

Do You Believe In Magic?

Sara was not sure she believed in magic. She did believe in synchronicity and serendipity, in fate and destiny, in karma and retribution. But she was not sure about the whole magic thing. Her mom was a big believer, but her dad was a scoffer. Her sister was a Christian and equated magic with the devil's work. Her brother was into sports and only believed in statistics.

So Sara was of at least two minds about the whole magic thing, perhaps even more than two. She did not feel that she "fit in" with the world as it was though. All through high school she had tried on different personas, like different hats. One year she was a Goth, hulking and skulking around the outer peripheries of the hallways, dressed in black, with heavy black eye makeup. She was sure, once people saw her skulking and hulking, they would leave her alone, but then a bunch of other Goth kids tried to spark her up and get her to join in their Goth group, but she was not interested. She actually *recoiled* from people that seemed attracted to her.

Another year she pretended to be a stoner, dressed in ripped jeans, a Bob Marley t-shirt and let her hair get all ratty. It was not actually dreadlocks but the closest thing she could get to them, without going all the way. Of course, that backfired as well, with the stoners constantly asking if she had a joint. Once she had gone with them to the back of the school and tried to smoke one that someone else offered her but had such a coughing fit that everyone got scared she was going to die and ran away, lest they get involved with her untimely demise.

Finally, she just gave up and decided to just be herself, which interestingly, did the trick. Everyone left her alone after that. Somehow, she had given off such a negative vibe that even the sports kids, who did not usually pick up on such things, were rebuffed.

She passed her high school years, alone but not too lonely, if that were possible. Sure, sometimes she got a *bit* lonely, but then she would remind herself that she liked it that way, or so she thought.

One day, she was roaming around the downtown area of her town. It was not really much of a downtown, as it was not really much of a town, but she liked it that way. She was slouching down the street and suddenly smelled an odd kind of smell. At least it seemed odd at the time. At the very least, it was not a smell she was used to smelling on that dingy, small-town street. But smell it she did, and she followed her nose down an alley, one that she did not remember seeing before.

She followed it until she came up to a small red door. It was not much bigger really, than the door that Alice had gone through in that long ago story that she had loved so long ago. So she stopped at the door and sniffed it a little, to make sure that it was the origin of the strange smell, and it was.

She tried to open the door, steeling herself, in case something jumped out at her. But nothing did, as the door did not open. Then she tried knocking, at first tentatively, then full on. For some reason, she was determined to get past this stupid little red door. But no one came and no one opened, and she just stood there, fuming. "Fuck," she said aloud, a few times "fuck, fuck, fuck."

She tried kicking the little door but that did no good and she only stubbed her toe on the unforgiving and unmoving door. "Fuck," she said again, and turned to go.

Suddenly, without warning, the door opened, very slowly, like a door in a horror movie, though at least it didn't make that horrible creaking sound like doors in the horror movies do. Sara peered into the space made by the now-open door but could see no one. "Shit", she said, "shit, shit, shit."

But she decided to go into that dark space that the door at made. What the hell, she thought. Why not? She entered the space slowly, a little at a time, until she was all the way into it and found herself in a long, rather dark corridor. Just like Alice, she thought. She hoped she wouldn't meet some creepy Cheshire Cat or have her head lopped off by a psychotic queen.

She moved on down the corridor, every cell in her body alive to threat or attack, but nothing happened and she found herself in a kitchen at the back of what seemed like a Chinese restaurant. Wait a minute, she thought, there was no Chinese restaurant in her town. She would know, because that was the only type of restaurant she liked, though she seldom got to go to one, unless her sister took her on Sunday, after church, which of course, she hated (the church part) out on the edge of town.

But she always liked the weird Chinese food, though she imagined that it was actually more like American Chinese food, seeing as they were in a small, boring town in Middle America. She even liked to eat with the two small pieces of wood that apparently Chinese people used with ease, though she found them damn irritating. But she had practiced with them at home, after pocketing hers after dinner, and she got pretty good at them. Her sister used to laugh at her, while eating her own *chow mien* with a fork, "like normal, American people did."

Anyways, here she was in the back room of a kitchen of a Chinese restaurant, which, as far as she knew, did not exist. That worried her for a moment, but then she mentally and physically shrugged and thought, what the hell, at least it's more interesting than the usual bullshit of her homely hometown.

There were racks and racks of pots and pans and piles and piles of dishes and bowls but no people. It was eerily quiet. Where were all the Chinese cooks, cooking and baking and yelling and swearing at each other, as she imagined a kitchen of a Chinese restaurant would be like? The stoves were all cold, and the ovens were all open and empty. Must be closed, she thought. She decided to check out the dining area.

She found a door that swung on its hinges, just like the restaurant doors she had always seen in movies. It even had a little round window on it, just like those movie doors. She pushed on it and it swung open easily, almost excitedly. She looked into the vast room, full of round tables and around the edges, a few booths, but no one seemed to be here either. She had just turned around to go back into the kitchen when she suddenly spied someone sitting in the very last booth, in the far corner of the room.

There were not very many lights on the in the room and the corner booth was pretty dark but there was definitely someone sitting there, and they seemed to be waving at Sara. Whoa, she thought, who the fuck is that? She hoped it wasn't a psychotic queen or something. But the person was waving so enthusiastically and had such a big smile on their face, she was reminded for a moment of that creepy Cheshire Cat but, after all, this was Middle America and nothing like that ever happened here, so she thought, so she hoped.

She found herself waving back, though she did not remember lifting her arm. Fuck it, she thought, I might as well go see who it is. She ducked briefly into the kitchen first though, and picked up a big carving knife, just in case.

She made her way slowly across the dimly lit room. As she got closer to the table, she saw that it was a little old man, like really little, like he had come from Alice's wonderland. It was then that she noticed the other people at the table, if you could call them that. One had such big

Chapter Four

ears that they kind of stuck up behind their head. Another had a small twitchy nose and big sleepy eyes. The old man who had waved at her so gaily across the room was wearing some kind of large, tall hat, like the one Honest Abe wore.

What is this? she thought. Who are these strange people? But they all seemed so friendly and invited her to sit down with them and have some tea. So, she sat down, while keeping a firm hold on her knife, which she held behind her back, just in case.

The little old man with the big hat was holding a teapot in his tiny hands and, smiling at Sara, poured some tea into a cup, splashing half of it over the table and held it out to Sara with a big smile. "Please my dear," he said, in a funny, high voice, "have some tea. It is really the very best!"

The other two people smiled at her with such warm and friendly smiles, she decided to go along, at least until she felt threatened. The one with the funny ears nodded his head and the one with the twitchy nose, started nodding off. His little head almost fell into his teacup, which was enormous, more like a tea bowl really. But the large-eared one grabbed him up at the last minute and slapped him in the face. "Wake up, you dolt. You almost drowned in your tea bowl!" To which the sleepy head smiled and said, "It's alright. I can hold my breath for ages!"

Sara laughed in spite of herself, in spite of her nervousness, and she felt herself relax and didn't even notice when she dropped the knife onto the floor. They were just all so cute and amusing and really very silly. She tasted her tea and indeed it was very good, probably the best she had ever tasted and then held her cup out for more.

"She wants some more," shouted the big eared one. "She wants some more," shouted the twitchy nose one. "Well then," shouted the big hatted one, "she shall have some more!"

Sara sat and drank numberless cups of excellent tea and laughed at their silly jokes and felt more at home with these strange little people that she had ever felt among anyone before. The time just slid by and she really had no idea what time it was or even what *day* it was. It was as if she had been sitting here, drinking tea, and laughing for hours, perhaps days.

But the little people started winding down, as if they were wind-up toys and their gears had run out. First Twitchy Nose had nodded off, though Big Ears quickly slid his tea bowl from under him. Then Big Ears nodded off, mumbling and bumbling a little in his sleep. Then High Hat's head drooped and drooped onto his little chest, though all the while, he kept mumbling, "Please have some more tea dear, it's really the very best.

Finally, she was left alone with three sleeping figures. She sat there for a while, enjoying their presence, even while they were unconscious. Then she slowly got up and crossed the big dining room, which was quite dark now and into the kitchen and then down the corridor and out of the little red door and out into the previously unknown alley.

Of course, when she went to visit her new tea friends the next day, she could not even find the alley, never mind the strange restaurant/teahouse. But, strangely enough, that didn't bother her. She felt that she had received some sort of transmission from them and that was good enough for her.

After that she relaxed a little and began to enjoy her life a little more. Gradually, she even made some friends, which pleased her. Of course, she never mentioned the funny tea party, but it seemed that its magic, if that is what you want to call it (which she did), had rubbed something off on her that stayed. And for that she was, dare she say, happy.

Chapter Five

The Banished Immortal

It was a cold and wet night, and the traveler was cold, wet, and very thirsty. He had been traveling for some time, enroute to a faraway part of the empire, banished once again by the Emperor. Once again, he had not been able to keep quiet in the August Presence. Maybe it was the wine, maybe it was just his character. Most probably the latter. Wine was a daily part of his existence after all, but keeping quiet when he saw someone being wronged was something that had gotten him into trouble many times.

When he was younger, he had studied sword with a master, an old Daoist hermit he had met on one of his mountain wanderings. For a while he had traveled all over the country as a "knight errent," helping people who needed help and getting rid of people who needed getting rid of.

He had written many poems about his wandering; many of them put to music by his many admirers. He was quite famous, even revered.

It was the glorious Tang, when culture and arts were held in very high esteem, from the Emperor on down to the lowest wine server. He had sung or recited his poems all over the empire, had written them on walls of many wine houses, and had even recited for the Emperor himself.

Actually, that is what had gotten the Emperor so angry with him that he had been banished to the far edge of the Tang Empire. He had a bad habit of speaking his mind in front of his "betters," those who lived at a much higher station than he did. But when he saw something wrong, it was just his first urge to speak up about it. So he did, and the Emperor was angered and, even worse, the Empress had been angered. Many a critic had lost their head over that. He was lucky he was only banished.

He often referred to himself as the Banished Immortal, as if he was one of those Immortals that the Daoists loved so, and had been sent down to the earthly realm, there to suffer like other humans. Yet, truth be told, he often thought of himself as more than human. How was it that he could make up such wonderful poems on a moment's notice, often while quite drunk on wine? Give him any topic at all and he could come up with verse and image and even rhythm and cadence, immediately. Many nights he had spent in lowly wine houses or the palaces of nobles, and was called upon to publicly spout his poems, like he was some kind of performing animal.

But now he traveled hard, accompanied by two stern guards, sent with him to make sure he went all the way to his new home, out on the marshy and pestilence-filled wilderness. He supposed they didn't feel any better than he did. He was sure they were as cold and wet and even thirsty as he was.

When the inn suddenly appeared, like a ghost through the fog, he thought it might be a mirage at first. But the closer they got to it, he saw that it was indeed an earthly inn, though he was a bit disappointed in that. He would have quite enjoyed sojourning at a ghost inn, and he was sure his guards would be quite disturbed, which he would have enjoyed. He knew that the average soldier was quite superstitious. He would have enjoyed watching them suffer while waited upon by ghostly servants.

He himself has come upon many ghosts in his wanderings in the mountains. He had once spent an entire evening with one. He had been sitting close by a small fire in a dark evening, when the stars were in hiding and the moon was absent. Suddenly he had felt a presence beside him, like a cold breeze blowing over him. Ah, he had thought to himself, I am in the presence of a spirit. But he had felt no evil presence, and decided it was just some lonely ghost, taking pleasure in his worldly fire.

They had spent the whole night there together, under the ink black sky, in the quiet of the mountains, which loomed over them both. He had offered some of his precious wine to the ghost but received no answer, for which he was grateful, as he hated to share what little wine that was left in his gourd.

The two of them sat in silence until the sun began rising, casting shadows all about them, though his ghostly companion cast no shadow. He could feel that the spirit was very sad and a bit lonely out here in the mountains. Perhaps he or she had been banished to that place, just as he was now banished away from "civilization," out to the place where the wild men and woman lived, who ate their meat raw, dressed in furs and spoke an unintelligible language.

As they got closer to the building, he noticed a rough signboard that said, "The Teahouse At The Edge Of The World" in crudely-written characters.

Doubly disappointed now, as it seemed that not only was it not a ghost inn but a teahouse, which in all probability did not serve wine. He was of course, as any cultivated man in the Middle Kingdom, greatly interested in fine teas. But, by the looks of the sign, it would probably be a rough and low-quality tea that he would be served this night.

With an audible sigh, he walked up to the gate of the inn, followed by his two guards, who were still not sure themselves if this might a haunted inn. The gate creaked open and suddenly a woman appeared, as if out of nowhere. She came so close to him that he took a step back, thinking she might be some kind of apparition.

But she smiled, showing white even teeth, rare in someone so old. She did seem very old to look at. The lines in her face were more like gullies or ditches, no doubt worn into her face by much sadness and suffering.

But her smile was very bright and looked much younger than the rest of her face. It was almost like a young person smiling behind the face of an old person!

"Welcome, "said the young/old woman. "Please come in." Then, she added, "You are most welcome here." And she said it in such a warm and friendly way, that he did feel very welcome indeed.

She seemed to glide an inch or so off the ground as she guided them into the inn. But the fog was so thick that he decided it was an illusion.

They entered a large room, full of small low tables, with rectangular cushions before each one. No one else seemed to be there, though the large room did feel as if it were full of people. "Spirits," he thought, or at least hoped.

The young/old woman led them to a table in a back corner of the room. The Banished Immortal looked about him and smiled. The guards however, were strangely and uncharacteristically quiet. He had gotten used to their loud, crude voices, entertaining each other about their exploits in the low class brothels of the capital. Of course, he had thought, they had never been in one of the high-class brothels, where some of the women had been imported from the far western reaches of the empire, where he himself had been born and brought up.

The old/young woman had disappeared somewhere in the back of the room and the three of them were left alone for quite some time. The soldiers grew impatient and started shouting for "service," but the Banished Immortal sat quietly, savoring the time out of the wind and cold and rain. He held his hands over the small charcoal brazier that sat in the center of the table and thought about what he could have done to appease the Empress and avoid this tiresome journey but could think of nothing.

I guess it is just my destiny, he thought to himself, to anger Her Highness in such a way as to get me sent from the very center of the world (Chang An) and out to the wild wilderness at the very edge of the world, which is where I presently sit, here on a cold and wet night with only two rustic buffoons for company.

If only I had been able to keep my mouth shut, he thought. By then again, he never had. That was his greatest failure, but also what he considered one of his best qualities. He was destined, he believed, for great things, yet it was his own fault that, instead of living out his days in opulence and luxery, he was sitting here in this ghostly inn, on his way to some far away marshland, there to probably die of some marshy fever.

Eventually the young/old woman came in with a teapot and three tea bowls, though once he looked closely at the tray she was carrying, he saw that there were four tea bowls. Odd, he thought, does this mean she is planning on joining us?

No, it seemed that fate really had in in for him this time. He was no longer allowed a sword. He was not even allowed to carry paper and ink on his banishment journey and his voice, which was his real weapon, had been silenced, at least for now. Oh well, his poems were many and beloved by many and he knew they would live on, long after he left this world of dust (as indeed they would.)

But for now, he would have to disregard his deep thirst for wine and be content with tea. The young/old woman sat down at the table and gave one of her girlish smiles. "This tea I have brought you" she said, "is a very special one, and has an interesting story behind it. It comes from a very special mountain, not far from here."

"It is said that once a poor woodcutter became lost in the forest near this mountain," began the woman. "Night began to fall, and he began to be very afraid because, as everyone knows, the night brings on the shadow people, those restless ghosts that roam about the forest at night. Of course, most of them are completely harmless, just sad remnants of a life filled with grief and sorrow, so that, even after death, the person, or ghost, still has that feeling of sorrow.

"But, in truth, if they would just let go of their sorrow, which does them no good in the spirit world, and can be released very easily there, they would find themselves free of all sorrow and grief and can just live in the spirit world as happy, light spirits. But some hold on to their sorrows and grief as if they were precious things. Then they become dark spirits and haunt the area in which they lived and harass the people living there. But actually, their power is not great, and they cannot really harm anyone, just scare them.

"The woodcutter, though not very educated, knew all of this. But it was still very frightening to hear the sound of these sorrowful ghosts flying by him, sending shivers through his entire body. There were also lots of awful sounds of moaning and groaning, which made all the hair on his body stand up on end.

"It was very dark in the forest and the poor woodcutter began to panic. Then he saw a light just up ahead. At first, he thought it might be the hut of a forest dweller or perhaps a woodcutter, like himself. But as he got closer, he found that the light was coming from a tree, a tea tree to be precise.

"And for some reason, he felt safer there by the tea tree, as it emitted its soft light into the surrounding darkness. He sat on the ground, right under the tea tree and passed the night there. In the morning he bowed to the tree in gratitude for protecting him all through the dark night. The light from the tree had dimmed greatly in the daylight and it only emitted a soft glow.

"He decided to take some of the leaves of the tree home with him, to remind him of the wonderful gift that the tree had given him. Now that it was light, he found his way back home quite easily.

"He put the leaves he had gathered out into the sun to dry and that evening, he brewed them in a clay pot. When he drank the tea, he felt so refreshed that he did not go to bed that night but instead stayed up and sang many songs, songs that he had learned in his youth and had not sung in many years. They were songs about the earth, about the mountains, about the rivers, about the animals in the forest and the trees there. (After all, he *was* a woodcutter.)

"There were songs that he had learned as a child, from his grandmother and grandfather, and his mother and father, even from his older sister, who was a wonderful singer. The woodcutter had never considered himself to be a good singer and was usually very shy about it.

"But that night he sang and sang, singing every song he had ever learned and even made up some more! When morning came, he was still not tired and so went off to the forest to cut his wood, singing all the way. Everyone in the village was amazed that this usually quite taciturn person had seemed to change his personality so much and so quickly!

"Before this, his life motto had been, "*chi ku,*" or "eat bitter." He seemed to think that life would always be bitter and hard and there was no use in thinking any other way. But now he sang and laughed all the time and seemed so happy and at ease with himself and the world around him.

"Of course, this made the villagers very curious and even a bit nervous. They talked amongst themselves and wanted to know what strange kind of magic had changed their bitter eating woodcutter into the happy, songster that he now was.

"Some of them decided to spy on him and see what was really going on with their neighbor. So that night, a few of them went to his house and peeked in through a large opening in the shutters. His hut, just all like the others in the village, consisted of only one room so it was very easy for them to see what was going on in it.

"They saw the woodcutter sitting wearily in front of his stove, looking off into space. He seemed so tired and so listless that it looked like he was about to nod off completely. Then he suddenly took a teakettle off his stove and poured hot water into a small clay teapot. He waited a few short moments and then drank it. Right away his whole being seemed to change. He leaped up from his stool and began to dance about the room, singing in a very loud voice.

"The neighbors could not help themselves, but knocked on his door, eager to find out what was in the tea he was drinking. The woodcutter came to the door and, when he saw that it was his neighbors, he invited them to try his amazing tea, which was just what they had been hoping for!

"He gave them each a small amount of the precious tea. He told them that it was from a very special magical tea tree that he had discovered when lost in the forest. But when he had tried to find it again, he was unable to and so only had a small amount of leaves left. But the tea was so powerful that after a few sips his neighbors felt their qi rise wonderfully in their bodies and their spirit become so light and free that they all joined in on the dancing and the singing.

"After that the whole village got to join in on the merriment as the woodcutter shared his magical brew with everyone. He still had to be very careful with the leaves, as he only had a finite amount of them. But it took so little of the magical tea for everyone to feel uplifted and lightened in spirit and body that it lasted quite a long time.

"And the most amazing part is that even when he ran out of leaves, the whole village continued to feel a sense of joy in their being. They would gather around a large bonfire in the center of the village on each full moon and each new moon and, even without the tea, they sang and danced joyfully into the night."

The woman stopped here and looked at the Banished Immortal. "Somehow," she said, "and I can't tell you how, I have managed to get my hands on a small amount of this wondrous tea, and I have been waiting for some time for the right person to come by that I can share it with."

Oh boy, thought the Banished Immortal, now we find out how incredibly expensive this tea is going to be for her "special" customer. But instead, the woman, as if reading his heart, said, "I will not charge you anything for this tea. I see that you are a man of cultivated spirit. I do not know from where you came and to where you are going, but I do know that this tea will help you on your journey."

The Banished Immortal was moved, almost to tears at this. It had seemed that he had lost all connection to civilization with his banishment. He wanted to try this marvelous tea right away but the woman said, "No, it is not for now. Keep it until you really need it, when you feel you have lost all hope. Then it will begin its magic upon you."

The soldiers were also all for brewing it up right away, but the women turned to them and said, "It is not for you!" in such a fierce voice that they lowered their heads and were quiet.

Then the woman made them some very fine tea, as fine as in any upscale teahouse the Banished Immortal had visited in the capital. Though not particular magical, it did seem to relieve their spirits and they passed the night in a warm glow and went on their way in the morning, with many bows to the woman and to the teahouse itself, with its odd name.

The Banished Immortal did live for many more years and wrote many more poems and could often be seen, dancing and singing, long before others had gone wearily to bed. It is said that he met his end while attempting to embrace the reflection of the full moon as it danced on the surface of a lake that he was boating upon. Many people were sad about this but those who were there said he had such a big smile upon his face as he sank into the depths of the lake that they felt it was more of a homecoming than a death.

The poet Li Bo or Li Bai, also known as the Banished Immortal, would live on as one the most beloved poets in Chinese history. Even today, many people know his poems and can recite them at the drop of a hat. Here is one of his most famous, possibly written during one of his banishments, translated by my friend Red Pine.

Thoughts on a Quiet Night

Before my bed the light is so bright
it looks like a layer of frost
lifting my head I gaze at the moon
lying back down I think of home

Chapter Six

The Teahouse For Ghosts

The idea of a teahouse for ghosts has been around for a long time. Most modern people think it is a myth, but it has a basis in real reality. Ghosts may not be able to drink tea, but they enjoy inhaling the fragrances of tea. It seems to cheer the sad ones, uplift the down-spirited ones, and relax the stressful ones.

You may not think of ghosts of being happy or sad or stressed out, but it true. They suffer many of the same things they suffered in life. The one's who left this world in sadness and fear still have a trace of that sadness and fear in their ghostly bodies. And the people who are too stressed out to enjoy life have the same problems on the other side.

The worst are what are called the "hungry ghosts." These hungry ghosts find themselves in the afterlife in a ghost body with tiny little mouths and thin little necks and huge swollen bellies, which they try to fill with tasty ghost food but, because of their tiny mouths and thin throats, they can barely swallow anything, and their suffering is endless.

These are most often people who behaved like hungry ghosts in their life, always wanting more, more, more. Always unsatisfied with what they had and never content with where they were and always looking over their shoulders so that no one would take what they had away.

These kinds of ghosts especially like coming to a ghost teahouse, because they don't have to worry about actually drinking the tea, but just get to enjoy small sniffs of it.

Ghost teahouses are usually situated in remote areas or can also be in the middle of a large city. Of course, no one who is not a ghost will ever find them, or even come across them accidently. Sometimes a ghost will enjoy the ghost teahouse so much that they remain there for years, even hundreds of years. It can get a bit crowded in ghost teahouses that have too many of this "hangers on," and sometimes the owners need to shoo them away.

Some of the ghosts who get kicked out of ghost teahouses get very irate and may even put up a fight, but the owners of these establishments are very tough and it is rare for any irate ghost to win.

Some ghosts get so attached to certain teas and tea fragrances that they spend all their time looking for the next "hit" of that tea. Sometimes it is a mild flowery green tea, or a fruity red tea, or a rich black tea. Some ghosts will only inhale well-fermented puerh tea. Whatever it is, instead of spending time studying their karmic destiny, and thereby being able to successfully reincarnate, they waste their valuable ghost lives in searching for their next "tea fix," and so never get to reincarnate, or else incarnate as a lower life form, like a cow or a pig.

As people have been drinking tea for thousands of years, so too have ghosts been sniffing it just as long. Sometimes, when we are sitting down to savor a nice hot cup of tea, we find that the tea has lost its flavor and may think we have brewed it wrong or that the tea is too old. But the real cause is that a ghost has been sniffing the tea before we get to taste it.

The reason for this is that not all tea-loving ghosts are in ghost teahouses, but sometimes they roam around the world of the living and "sponge" off them, taking the best parts of tea when we are not looking. It is hard to find fault with this practice as they, in their ghostly forms, get to enjoy so little.

It is not easy to be a ghost, especially for one who is just a hairwidth apart from the living world. Some ghosts spend their time deep, deep in the spirit world and have no interest or need to interact with living people. Others may spend their time just barely on the other side and are still very affected by things in the world of the living. Some of them may not even know they are ghosts and become very frustrated in their attempts to interact with the world of the living.

But some may be vengeful ghosts who are holding a grudge against someone in the living world or just against the living world in general. These kinds of ghosts waste a lot of time trying to "get even" with someone in the living world.

Other kinds of ghosts are those who are very sad and pining away for their past selves, when they thought they were so happy, or imagined they were so happy. These kinds of ghosts also waste a lot of time trying to reconnect with loved ones, often causing a lot of problems with the living, and are rarely satisfied with the results.

The beings who run the ghost teahouses are, of course, ghosts themselves. But they are very old ghosts. You might even call them Bodhisattva ghosts. In other words, they could have incarnated again, but have decided to hold off and stay a ghost in order to serve other ghosts. Why they do this, no one knows. All we know is that they stay at the ghost teahouse, running the whole show, so that other ghosts can come and find a little bit of pleasure in their ghostly lives.

Many of the ghosts who frequent the ghost teahouses were lovers, and even connoisseurs, of tea in their life. On their deathbed, one of the things they felt they were going to miss most was the deep pleasure of drinking tea. But once they find their way to the ghost teahouse, they find that, though they cannot drink the tea, just sniffing the tea and letting the fragrance and sometimes, even the qi of the tea enter their ghostly bodies, is almost as good.

As previously mentioned, one cannot purposely find these kinds of teahouses. Just like the Teahouse At The Edge Of The World, even a ghost cannot just follow a map or any kind of directions to find this type of teahouse. Instead, they have to just "come upon it." Asking for guidance is fine but asking for direct directions is not. These ghost teahouses are often located out on the edge of the world, or you could say, in the world between worlds.

After all, if they were one hundred percent in the ghost world, where would they get their tea? The ghosts who run the ghost teahouses are able to travel into the world of the living and pick the tea leaves in the early, early morning, before the earliest of the early pickers arrive.

Then they carry the glistening leaves back to the ghost teahouse and brew it up in huge cauldrons of hot water. The tea-loving ghosts who have found their way to the ghost teahouse usually line up at the door of the teahouse early in the morning, eager to enter and begin sniffing the wonderful tea.

Of course, in the ghost world, there is no such thing as morning or afternoon or even evening. It is all one time to the ghosts there. But the tea-loving ghosts like to think of the time they line up at the door of the teahouse as early morning, because that was when they used to start their day with their little tea ceremonies when they lived in the land of the living.

So if you are a tea lover and are lying on your deathbed and bemoaning the fate of not being able to drink tea ever again, be sure when you get to the other side, to look around for a ghost teahouse. And if you find your way to one, you will not be disappointed.

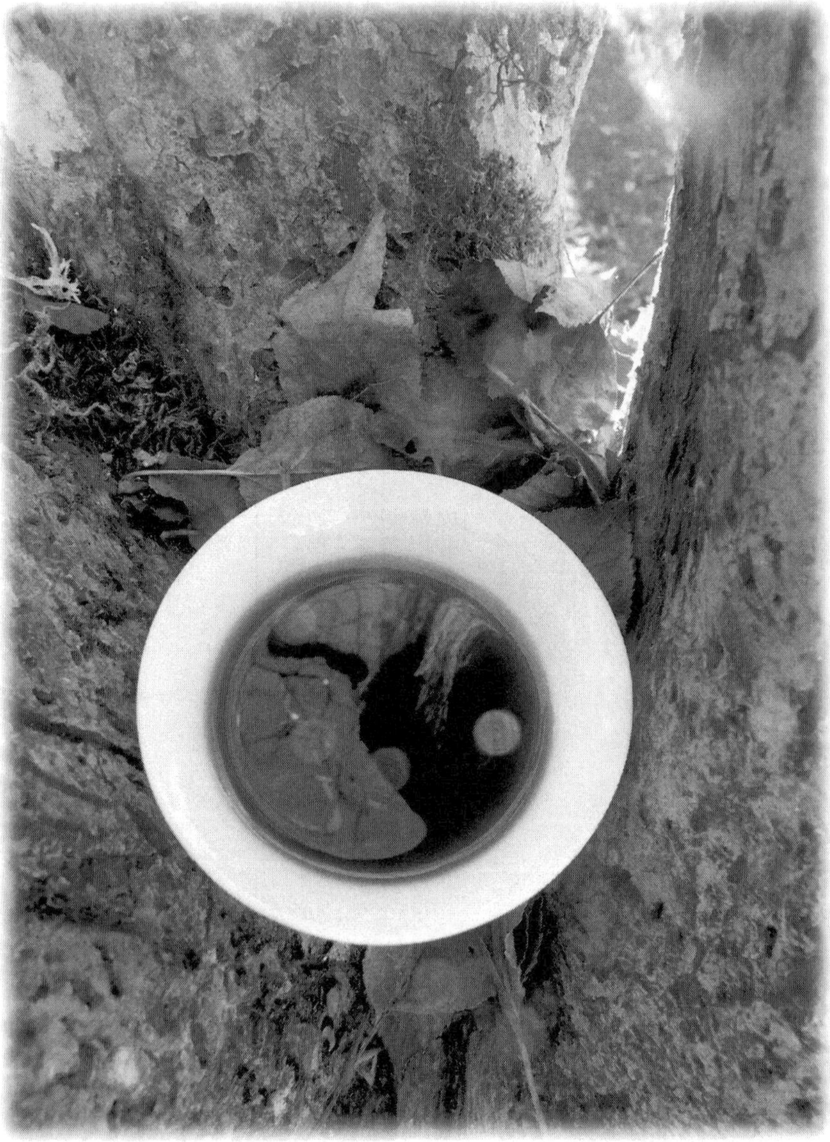

Chapter Seven

The Boy With Stones For Eyes

The boy with stones for eyes was, unfortunately, born that way. When he first whooshed out of his mother's womb, like a fish falling out of a fish basket, the midwife took one look at him and fainted dead away.

And when the recovered midwife placed the baby in his father's arms, *he* took one look at him and immediately dropped him to the floor. The baby began complaining, vigorously and loudly.

But when the midwife laid him in his mother's arms, his mother took one look at him and fell in love immediately. She did not seem to mind that her baby had stones for eyes. She thought he was the most beautiful baby she had ever seen. She smiled at him, and he stopped crying and smiled back, almost as if he could see her, with his stony eyes.

Of course, as he grew up to become a boy, all the other boys and even some of the girls made fun of him. They teased him unmercifully, running all around him and shouting him, laughing at him, pushing him, and even pinching him!

But the boy with stones for eyes never cried, even when they pushed him into a big pile of pig shit. Maybe it was because he had those stones for eyes or maybe it was that he was such a mild mannered and happy boy, even with his strange affliction.

He would just smile at the taunting children and never complain and never cry. This would drive the bullies crazy but, no matter how much they tormented him, he would never show any anger or even sadness. He would just turn around and walk slowly to his home, where his mother, who continued to love him and see him as the most beautiful boy in the world, would welcome him with open arms.

She was very sad about the bullying and held him close, as if she could shield him from all the bullies of the world. But alas, the world is filled with bullies, even grown-up ones.

The years went on and the boy grew older and larger, so large that the bullies stopped bullying him. Though he never seemed to mind their bullying, they were afraid that one day he would, and he was so large and so obviously strong, that they were afraid of him.

He was so strong because his father who, truth to tell, was more than a little ashamed of him, would take him out to the forest each day to cut firewood, which is how he made his meager living.

They would spend all day cutting up and stacking the wood and at the end of the day, would pile the wood onto a little cart and drag the cart back to the village. As the years went by, the boy with stones for eyes got stronger and stronger and was able to carry bigger and bigger loads of wood, and the father began to make more money, and also began to feel, almost begrudgingly, a little proud of his strange looking son.

No one knew just how the boy saw the world, through those stony eyes. In some ways, he seemed like a blind person, carefully feeling his way through the world, but at other times, it seemed as though he could actually see the world through those strange eyes, though what it looked like to him, no one could say.

Sometimes his mother would ask him what the world looked like to him and he would say things like, "It's all bright and shiny," or, "Everything looks like it's made of stone, even the people."

"Even me?" she would ask, afraid of what he might say. But her beautiful boy would turn his head toward her and smile and say, "Everyone but you mother. You look like what I think the sun must look like."

Eventually, the boy grew into a man and his parents grew into an old man and an old woman and eventually they left this world and the boy, who was now a man, was left alone. But he didn't seem to mind. He just acted like had always acted and went through the village, smiling at everyone he met. Some people thought he might be simple minded, but he was not, just simple hearted.

Some of the people were a little afraid of him, and some of them liked him very much, and some of them even loved him, but they could never guess just why he was born with stones for eyes and just how did he see the world around them all.

After some more long years, the boy with stones for eyes, who was now a man with stones for eyes, disappeared from the village. No one knew where he had gone or why. After all, he had lived in the tiny village of his birth for a long, long time and everyone knew him there, and he knew everyone, and could walk through the village without feeling his way.

But he had gotten tired of his tiny village, and he decided to go out and see the wide world, though what this wide world looked like to him, no one can say. But leave he did, and after bowing deeply to the memory of his father and his beloved mother, he turned his head towards the sun and began walking.

He walked and walked, for a long time until he came to a river.

Though he could not see the river, or at least he could not see the river the way most people see a river, he could certainty hear it and could certainly smell it. It smelled like fish and plants and water and a little like his beloved mother. So, he stood and smiled at the river and he could feel the river smile back at him.

Then he smelled smoke and liked the warm way it smelled and felt, and he decided to go and see where it was coming from. So he turned his stony eyes toward the smoky smell and began walking. After a short while, he found himself in front of a small building. It was made of old wood, worn smooth and even shiny, it was so old. And there was a short little chimney at the top of the building, which was breathing forth clouds of smoke.

He went to the door opening of the building and knocked, saying, "Hello there, you smell good!"

For a few minutes there was no sound from the door opening, and he began to turn to go when suddenly a voice cried out, though very softly, "Please come in good sir, and have some tea."

He had often sat and enjoyed tea with his mother, but since she had died, he had not done so and when he heard the word "tea" he smiled and entered the building.

He sat himself down on a low cushion right in front of the little fire, which was dancing merrily under a kettle of water. The water smelled even better than the river water and he began to get excited about what was going to happen.

He thought about the word "tea," and it almost sounded as good as the word "mother."

The person who had been speaking all the while he had sat himself down and thought his thoughts of tea and mother, kept on speaking but also, began to make some tea.

"Ah," thought the man with stones for eyes, "maybe this person is the Mother of Tea."

Indeed, it was the Mother of Tea, who lived in that special building, which was actually The Teahouse At The Edge Of The World!

The Mother of Tea kept talking, all while she prepared the tea. He did not exactly listen to what she was saying, but just let her voice wash over him like the music of the river, which had led him there, to The Teahouse At The Edge Of The World.

The sound of her voice was so soothing, so comforting, and so gentle. It sounded like the voice of his mother, when she would hold him when he was a baby and as a young child, and sing to him songs that she had learned in her own childhood, and which always felt like a soothing balm to his heart.

Whenever he had come home with clothes torn and a face covered with mud or pig shit, she would gather him up in her arms and wipe off his face and sing to him in a gentle and soothing voice, much like the Mother of Tea was using right now.

He smiled a big smile and he felt that smile wafting over to the Mother of Tea, floating like the smoke that gently lifted from the fire beneath the tea kettle, that was filled with the tea that she now served him, placing a small cup of warmly glowing tea into his hands.

He felt her smiling at him like the sun and he drank the tea, slowly and carefully, and felt the warmth of the tea flow through his body like a magical elixir.

Suddenly the Mother of Tea stopped speaking and just sat and looked at him for a long time, slowly nodding her head at him, as if she were approving of him, just like his mother had done so long ago.

"This tea," she suddenly said, "is a very special tea. It will not cure your eyes. I can see that you don't need curing. You are fine and well just the way you are. Your stone eyes show you the world as it truly is instead of the way most people see it. You see the beauty of the world, instead of the ugliness. That is your gift to the world. I am glad you have come here to visit with me and drink some of my special tea, because you are a very special person. Your mother knew this, even if the world did not know it.

"Your stone eyes can see into the deep truth of the world and how it really is, not just what it appears to be. You are happy because you accept the world as it is. You have always known this, even when you were bullied as a child. This is why the bullies could not really hurt you. Your spirit is so strong that they could not harm it. Your heart is so clear that the dirt of the world could not stain it."

She sat and smiled her big sun smile at him, and he smiled back. His stony eyes began to light up from deep inside. It was like they had transformed from stones to crystals and he could see all the light of the world rushing out to meet him, and for a moment he felt dizzy, and then he felt calm, and he held out his cup for more tea from the Mother Of Tea, there in the deep, deep forest by the dancing river, there at The Teahouse At The Edge Of The World.

Chapter Eight

The Floating Teahouse

There was once a poor man, who did not love being a poor man and instead, wanted, with all his heart, to be a rich man. His father was poor and his grandfather and his grandfather before him and all the way back as far as his family history went, had been poor.

Even as a child, he had longed to be rich. Everyone in his family, everyone in the village even, laughed at him. Of course, he was a poor child, they said, and would undoubtedly be a poor man. After all, was not everyone in his family and everyone in his village poor?

They lived in the south of China and so grew rice, which was back-breaking labor, bent over the fetid water, planting shoots, one after another, all day long, until you could hardly straighten your back at the end of the day. And the day after that and the day after that.

Of course, they grew a little plot of vegetables on the side. After all, no one could live just by rice alone. They needed cabbage and various other green things. They could only afford to eat meat at special times of the year, mostly on festival days. And so everyone in the village was very thin. All except for the landlord, of course. He was very fat and greasy and lecherous. The people of the village learned to hide their comely daughters when he came for the rent. He was so fat, he could hardly get on and off his horse. But they could see that he was not happy and certainly not healthy, wheezing and barely able, with the help of his servants, to mount his gigantic horse.

So, thought the people, we are better off. We may be poor, we may be thin, but we are strong and we do not wheeze when we walk.

But this one child, who grew up to be a man, still wanted, deep within his heart and soul, to be a rich man. He would not be fat when he was rich, he thought. He would not be greasy and lecherous and unkind. He would be a good rich man, a fair rich man, and only take enough to live on and leave the rest for the poor ones to fill their small bellies.

Over the years, he tried everything to get rich. He had all sorts of complicated, and sometimes even dangerous schemes, many of which he talked his friends into, all of which failed. So many times he *almost* made it, could see and feel and even taste it, this goal he so ardently and absurdly worked for, but in the end, was at least as poor as when he had started, if not more so.

Finally, he realized that there was no way he could become rich by working for it. He would have to take it, steal it if that is what was needed. So he became an outlaw. There were others who also wished to be rich and who also did not want to work for it. They banded together and lived in the marshes outside of the villages and plied their trade all along the roads leading to the surrounding villages. Of course, living in such a poor area, they could not steal much. After all, they were not *murderers*. They usually left a little, enough to live on, with the people that they stole from.

Of course, if there were any rich people on the road, well they were fair game and the outlaws stole everything they could from them, down to their underwear and shoes.

And so, this poor man, who never did become a rich man, even as an outlaw, just a little less poor, eventually realized that being an outlaw in this poor area would never result in him becoming a rich man. He decided to leave the band of outlaws and make his way to the big city, where he was sure he would strike it rich.

He snuck off from the band of outlaws in the middle of the night and made his way to the city. He had never seen so many people, animals, and buildings in one place before! At first he had a hard time breathing, the air was so full of smells and sounds and sights. He made his way to the poorest end of the city, to where he could afford a night in a poor inn. The inn itself was also so full of people and sounds and some not very good smells that he hardly slept a wink, lying next to other snoring and belching and farting men.

In the morning, after a meager breakfast of watery rice and even more watery tea, he made his way to the market area of the city. There he hoped to find work until he could become accustomed to the city and figure out a way to become rich. He found work that first day, but it was such back-breaking labor, unloading huge wagons of rice bales, that he was transported back to his days of planting rice in the village, and so he quit right after he got his meager wages for the day.

He tried to find other, less wearisome jobs, but could not. He soon spent what little cash he had and was reduced to begging by the side of the road. He sat there, just outside a temple to the goddess Guan Yin, begging for pennies or a handful of rice. He hoped that the fact that he was at the Goddess of Mercy's temple that people would be moved to help, but few did. Most of them passed him right by, as if he were invisible, which to them, he was. Or else they held their nose as they passed. It was true, he stank, but that was because he was so poor, and the poor cannot afford to go to the bathhouse. But after all, he was still a man. A man who had once had dreams, though they were all gone now, like smoke on the breeze.

Other beggars often came to this spot, thinking as he did, that the temple of the Goddess of Mercy would be a good place to beg. But they also found that it was not so, and so they did not come back. He was the only one there, until one day an old man hobbled over to a spot right next to him and held out his own withered hand to the people who passed by and ignored him.

But this man did not become angry, as the young man did, when the people passed them by and ignored them or held their noses. He just laughed, as if it were all a big joke.

Together, after a long day of begging, each man usually made enough, just enough, to keep them alive for one more day. One more day of begging and being humiliated.

But the old man did not seem humiliated and just laughed his rich laugh every time someone ignored his outthrust hand. Well, the young man thought, at least he is rich in laughter. But, as the days wore on and they continued to receive only enough to live one more day, he became curious about this other man, the one rich in laughter, if nothing else.

"*Shu Shu,*" said one day, using the honorific title of "uncle." He would have called him "*Ye Ye*" the term for "grandfather," but he didn't want to insult him by implying he was as old as he looked. "I watch you every day here, begging for pennies and receiving few. Yet every time the people pass you by and hold their nose, you laugh. What is there to laugh about here in our pitiful state?"

The old man turned to him and said, "Ah, *Zhi Zi,*" using an honorific for nephew, "like you, I am a beggar, but for me it is not so pitiful a life. True, I sit here all day and most people ignore me or pity me or are even repulsed by me, but that is not my concern. It truly does not have anything to do with who and what I really am."

"Who and what are you then?" the young man asked.

"I am a *Zhen Ren,*" said the old man, "an Authentic Person. I know who and what I am and what others think of me does not interest me. It certainly does not anger me. These petty people pass us by each day so that they can go in and worship the Goddess of Mercy and Compassion, the great Guan Yin. But Guan Yin does not hear their prayers and their supplications. Her heart is not moved to pity and compassion for them. To her, these people are not worthy of her grace.

"But you and I, my friend, are not to be pitied, especially by ourselves. We are free men and are not beholden to anyone for our daily rice. True, it is a small amount, and only enough to allow us to live another day, but this is where we choose to be and do and so it is good and right. And that is why I laugh, because, unlike these others, who are so bent down by their money troubles and their family troubles and their clan troubles, I am free and accountable to no one except my own self."

"But they eat all they wish every day," said the other one. "They sleep in soft beds and have many servants who they can order around as they wish. Even the poorest among them is richer than both of us put together. Is this not a pitiful thing?"

"No," said the old one, "not pitiful for us, though perhaps pitiful for them."

One day, after sitting all day under the hot sun and begging for pennies from the idle rich, the old one asked the young one if he wished to accompany him to a local teahouse. "But," said the young one, "we have received so little money today, how in this world are we to afford to drink tea? Is it not expensive?"

"No," answered the old one. "This teahouse I will bring you to is not expensive at all, and it is a very special teahouse."

"In what way?" asked the young one.

"I will show you," answered the old one. "It is better that you see with your own eyes and your own heart."

So, the poor young man and the equally poor old man, started on their way. They walked for long, long ways. Many times, he wanted to give up but the old one kept saying, "just a little more."

"This teahouse," said the young man at one point, "seems to exist on the outer edge of town."

"That may be," said the old man. "It is indeed very far, some say all the way to the edge of the world, but today it is just on the edge of town."

"Is this then a moving teahouse?" asked the young man.

"You will see," said the old man, and then would say no more.

On they trudged, with empty bellies and weak limbs, but at last, just when the young man began to give up, they came to the teahouse. It stood there, floating in the middle of a pond, all lit up like a dazzling flower. There was a small wooden bridge that traversed the pond and over it they went. To tell the truth, it looked to the young man as the fanciest, most fanciful whorehouse he had ever seen, and he felt the few small coins in his pocket and wondered if he had enough to buy a night's bliss.

But, once they entered through the round door, he found that it was indeed a teahouse, but not *just* a teahouse. It was the most amazing and loveliest building he had ever been in. It was not large but not small either. It seemed just the perfect size.

The old man seemed to be known there and they were quickly seated at a table right in the middle of the room, though the young man would had probably chosen one in the back. He looked around the room, gawking at the rich, though simple paintings he saw there, mostly exquisitely done landscapes, with tall mist-covered mountains at the top, then down to a full forest halfway down, and then all the way down to a simple and rustic teahouse on the very edge of a rushing river. And in the small teahouse he saw two people seated at a round table in the very middle of the room. The figures were so small he could not make out their faces, but something told him that he would recognize them right away if he could.

When he turned around, he saw that a small teapot and two very small teacups had appeared on the table. Next to them was a small yet elegant tea canister, which was filled with something so wonderfully fragrant that he forgot all about his empty belly, and instead found his head filled with visions of fairies and immortals. He felt that, even if he did not get to actually *taste* that tea he would still have experienced an amazing and wonderful journey!

Presently, the old man took a tiny amount of the fragrant tea from the beautifully decorated tea canister and dropped it into the small pot. Then he took up a kettle of water that sat at the edge of the table, where it sat on a bed of coals, bubbling quietly to itself, and poured it into the teapot.

"Now we must let the water and tea dance with each other for a small spell," he said. He sat back and smiled at the young man. "I too was amazed at this teahouse the first time I visited it," he said.

"But I have walked this way many times on my explorations of this city," said the young man, "and I never saw this place before. Is it very new?"

The old man did not answer but gently lifted the teapot and poured the tea into the two tiny cups. There seemed to be just enough tea in it to fill both cups. Then he presented one of them to the young man, holding the cup in both hands and giving a small bow.

The young man took the cup and raised it to his mouth, but before tasting it, he inhaled the rich fragrance, letting it fill his nose. It was unlike any tea he had ever smelled. Of course, being a poor man all his life, he had not often smelled high quality tea, but he had robbed enough rich men of their possessions, which often contained high quality tea, and so he knew what it smelled like. But *this* tea was different from any he had ever come across. The fragrance itself seemed alive, spreading from his nose into his whole being, traveling all the way into his belly.

Then he put the cup to his lips and let a small amount of the tea fill his mouth. Again, the tea felt like it was traveling throughout his whole body, filling it up from the bottom of his feet to the top of his head.

The old man sat and smiled at him while he drank a little more of the magical tea. Thus they sat for some time, drinking steeping after steeping of that wonderful tea. It seemed to be never ending, those countless steepings, until at last, the tea was played out and they had gotten all they could out of it.

They both sat there, each lost in his own thoughts and his own experience with the marvelous tea. The young man closed his eyes and felt as though, if he were to die on this one day, he would die a happy and contented man. He felt a sense of peace that he had never felt before. Suddenly, he felt that it did not matter if he was a poor man or a rich man or a happy man or a sad one. He was just who he was now, in this moment, and hopefully in the next. He was fine with who and what he was, in a way that he had never felt before. All those years of trying to become rich, he thought, such a waste of time.

At last, the old man stood up and motioned for the other to follow him out of the teahouse. The young man walked as if in a trance, for he was truly entranced by the whole experience of the tea and the teahouse itself. His feet seemed to travel a few inches above the ground, and he floated along as if he were walking upon a cloud.

Once they had crossed the little wooden bridge, he turned around for one last look at the magical teahouse but, to his confusion, the teahouse appeared to have disappeared. There was just the pond and a few ripples, flowing outwards, as if a stone had been thrown into the water. He wondered if the teahouse was some sort of enchantment but found that he did not care. Even if he were to not ever see or experience that enchanted teahouse again, he would still feel his life was changed because of that one short evening there.

After that, while begging alongside the old man, there were days when the Goddess of Mercy smiled on them, and their begging bowls would be filled. There were also days when She did not, and their outstretched palms remained empty. But, even so, the young man found that he could now laugh along with the old one when that happened.

Chapter Nine

The True Story of Jack and Jill

Once upon a time, in the deepest part of the forest, where only the wind came to play, there lived a boy and a girl. They were brother and sister in all the ways that were. They lived alone in a small cottage of their own. No one knew where they had come from or how they had gotten there. As far as anyone knew, they had always been there. They had one name each. The boy's name was Jack and the girl's name was Jill. They were happy and content and alone, and they were healers.

Every day, just at dawn, people would arrive at the little meadow at the edge of Jack and Jill's cottage. These people were sick or lame or filled with sadness and longing. They came to be healed. They came to be filled with joy and a reason to live. They came to receive.

And every day, just at dawn, when everyone was still and waiting, Jack and Jill would emerge from their cottage with a large pot of tea. Magic tea. Healing tea. But when people remarked about how special this tea was, the children would answer that the tea itself was not so special. It was the water they used that made it so.

Where it came from, no one knew. It was said that they got it from a secret well, hidden on some far-off hilltop, at the very far side of the forest. Many people had searched but no one had ever been able to find the well. It was hidden behind a cloud, and only Jack and Jill knew where to find it.

The children would carry the pot of healing tea down to the people, who waited in silence. The children smiled like sun gods and offered a small drink of the tea to each person they came to. Some people were cured right away. Others had to go home and wait awhile for the healing tea to take effect. But eventually, everyone was cured. Crippled limbs straightened out and took on new strength, fevers abated, blisters and sores disappeared, foggy brains cleared, deaf ears began to hear and the blind eyes to see. The sad and desolate became overjoyed at being alive. The rejected and lost found themselves again, in new ways, and the sullen and vengeful found a peace they had never known.

Some sought to reward the children but were gently refused. "Go in peace," they said to the tearful and thankful people. "We are only here to give, not to receive." Then the people blessed them and would have worshipped them, but again the children refused. "No," they said, "it is not we who heal. It is the water that the tea is made of, which is a gift through us to you. The gift is from the Earth herself, not us. We are only her servants. Now go your way and have a good life."

Then all the people would leave, filled with something more than they had been. The children would then retire into their little cottage to while away the day playing, singing, eating, and waiting for evening to come to beckon them to sleep.

Then, a little before the dawn, they would emerge from a hidden door and disappear into the forest. Somewhere they would plunge into the brush, push their way through, and climb up a steep path up a high hill, and draw from a secret well the healing water that they would use to make the tea that they would share with the people that day. No one knew what they said there, and no one ever saw them go. Except once.

Sometimes there were people who became jealous of Jack and Jill, who would envy them the love the people had for their healers. Same people, misguided and tortured in their own agony, wished that they too could be loved like that. There were some who would not have refused when the people wanted to reward them. There were some, so sad and empty inside, that they would have liked to have been worshiped as something more than they were.

One of these was Shagrag. Shagrag was a magician of sorts. By that I mean he was good at *causing* sickness rather than *curing* it. He was good at making people miserable rather than happy. He was good at creating disharmony around him rather than beauty.

Sometimes people would hire Shagrag when they wanted revenge on someone. Sometimes people used him when they wanted someone else to suffer. But they did not love him, and they certainly did not worship him. They usually wanted him to leave as soon as his wretched work was done. They did not invite him to sit and drink tea with them or relax with them in the shade and watch the children play on the grass. So Shagrag was lonely, and in his loneliness, he struck out at the very two whom he hated the most. Because they were so good, so selfless and so loved by everyone.

So he thought and thought in the deepest, darkest part of himself and he came up with a plan. One morning, he showed up at Jack and Jill's with his arm in a sling. He pretended to be in pain. He waited with all the others in the early predawn light. A cool mist hung over the meadow where everyone sat or lay on long, low benches, waiting for the children to come with the magic, healing tea. He sat and listened while everyone praised Jack and Jill and eagerly awaited their arrival, with smiles and laughter. Even the worst suffering of them were feeling better already. Shagrag winced and squirmed on his seat, feeling his anger and hatred grow and grow until there was no room inside of him for anything else.

Soon Jack and Jill came out of their cottage, bearing the pot of sacred tea. The people sat or lay quietly, each being served in turn. Sometimes

Jack or Jill would smile and speak a few words to someone. Sometimes people would cry out and hug them or kiss them. But when Shagrag's turn came, he looked away from their shining faces and spat the tea out when they had passed. The sweet, healing tea had tasted bitter and dirty to him.

Most of the people left after they had all been served, though a few stayed and lay about in the sun, feeling their new and strong bodies. Shagrag sat apart and watched the cottage all day to see if the children would come out and give any indication of where they got the water for their magical tea. But they never did, and finally, after the people left, Shagrag hid himself in the bushes and continued watching the cottage.

Eventually evening came, then the deepest part of the night, when the fairy and forest folk began their nightly romp through the meadow. The tree spirits and fauns danced together in the open, their voices mingling together in the air. But Shagrag saw none of this. He was too deeply imbedded in his own darkness to notice these beings of light.

The night passed and dawn drew near, and still there was no sign of the children. "Aha," thought Shagrag suddenly, "*of course* they would not just walk openly and lead someone to the secret well. There must be a hidden door." He closed his eyes, murmured a few dark and smoldering words, and slowly a faint picture came to him. Clearer and clearer it came, until at last he saw it, the hidden door! "Of course," he muttered, and ran around to the side of the cottage nearest the forest, just as the children emerged from it and disappeared into the brush.

Shagrag followed them a little way behind, very careful to make no noise as he crept through the underbrush. The children did not know he was there. He had hidden himself well in a dark mist and could not be seen. They were talking, in low quiet voices, which swirled round and round each other in the faint morning light. They held each other's hand and took turns carrying the empty jar.

Presently, they came to the far edge of the woodland at a place unmarked by any sign that Shagrag could see, where they plunged through the brush and out onto a path at the bottom of a steep hill. "At last," gloated Shagrag to himself. "They have led me to the well! Only a little longer and I shall have the secret of the healing water. Then I shall become beloved before all!"

The children started up the hill, still unaware of Shagrag following behind. Up and up they went, until they got to the very top, on which sat a small stone well, uncovered and ringed with flowers. Shagrag saw Jill bend over and fill the jar, hold it up to the sky, then pour a little water on the ground. She took a small drink and then handed the jar over to Jack. Now was his chance!

Shagrag leaped towards Jack from here he had been hiding in the tall grass. The children stood where they were, watching him come towards them. They didn't move or seem surprised. Shagrag slammed into Jack, almost knocking him over. The jar fell to the ground. Jack waved his arms wildly in the air, trying to regain his balance. At last, he pitched over and began to roll down the hill. Over and over, he turned, bounding off rocks and tree roots. Jill screamed once, then snatching the jar, ran after him. Shagrag, seeing her run off with the jar, ran after her.

Jill flew down to the bottom of the hill like a bird, leaving Shagrag far behind. When she reached the bottom, she found Jack lying all twisted and broken, his head bleeding and torn. She quickly raised his head a little and tried to pour a few drops of water into his open mouth, but her hands were shaking so hard she kept spilling the water down the side of this face. Finally, she took a little of the water into her own mouth. Then, closing her mouth onto Jack's, she slowly let the healing water drip from her mouth into his and slide down his throat. She did this several times and then sat back and watched him anxiously.

After what seemed a long time, Jack opened his eyes into hers and smiled a deep, full smile. His head stopped bleeding and he sat up.

It was then that Shagrag reached them. He was out of breath and sore where he had fallen and banged his knees a dozen times on his wild flight down the hillside. He snarled and picked up a huge stone to throw at them, when Jill did a most curious thing. She snatched up the jar and threw the water at him. It flowed down his head and into his beard and over his chest and down his legs and on the ground, where it made a little puddle at his feet.

For a while no one moved. Then Shagrag put down the stone. He made an odd little sound, then grimaced. Then he screamed. The water felt like fire, burning him all over. He screamed again and fell to the ground, rolling over and over in the grass, trying to put out the fire. He felt it burning through his skin and start on his insides. He cried out as it reached his secret and innermost dark places, burning them up with a roar.

Then, just as suddenly as it had come, the fire was gone. He sat up. The burning was gone and in its place was a gentle coolness like had never felt before. He felt light and airy, almost as if he would float away. His mouth tasted sweet, and his hands felt the earth beneath him in a gentle caress. He looked over at Jack and Jill, who were both standing now and smiling at him.

Jill picked up the empty jar and held out her hand to him. He took it and she lifted him up lightly. Together they turned, and without a word spoken, started back up the hill, where Jill once more filled the jar with the precious, healing water.

Shagrag felt like laughing. Then he felt like crying. Then he felt like singing. Then he felt like doing everything at once, and tried to, but he started choking and Jack had to slap him on the back. He looked around and saw all the trees nodding to him, all the flowers bowing to him, all the birds singing big hellos to him. The whole world around him seemed to be filled with praise and love for him. For him. "Why?" he thought. "I don't deserve it. I have never done anything to deserve this."

He turned to Jill. "But I don't deserve it," he said.

"Yes you do," she said, smiling at him.

"The world loves you," said Jack. "The Earth loves you. You don't have to do anything to deserve it. It just is."

"Even me?" asked Shagrag, feeling a bit guilty, after all he had done.

"Even you," said Jack.

"Even you," repeated Jill. "Now we must hurry if we are to arrive in time for the dawn. The people will be waiting."

And so it came to pass that a lonely, jealous person was made whole through the blessing of the tea and the water, the free gift of the Earth, though her servants, Jack and Jill. And it is said that ever after, when the people came to be healed, they would find one already there before them, helping them to their benches, soothing the fretful ones, reminding the forgetful ones, seeing to the suffering ones, joking with the frightened ones. And to anyone who cared to listen, he would tell his tale, that of Shagrag the dark magician, who, through the gift of the sacred water, became the servant of the servants.

Chapter Ten

The Teahouse At The Edge Of The World Sutra

Sophie had been a serious meditator for many years. By serious, I mean she took it very seriously and she kept up a very regular meditation schedule. Once in the morning, once again in the evening. At least 30-60 minutes each time. Had been doing it for years.

But she was beginning to get a little frustrated, as her meditation practice was not yielding much, compared to what she was putting into it. It was like depositing money over and over again into an account, but never seeing any return on it.

Of course, it was not like she was expecting enlightenment or anything like that. Maybe a little *satori* now and then would be nice though. A little glimpse into the vast depths of Dao. Sophie's practice was a blend of Daoism and Zen (which is itself a nice blend of Buddhist and Daoism) and Tibetan Buddhism.

She was also a studious student of various sutras. She had studied many sutras, from the Diamond to the Heart, and felt that she had a good grasp of their meaning and their meaning for her own life. But she still felt unfulfilled. Instead of being filled with wisdom and insight, she felt slightly adrift, bobbing slowly around in a sea of *samsara*.

Then, one slow moving, humdrum day, she found a brief allusion on one of the many Buddhist websites she frequented, to a very rare sutra, called The Teahouse At The Edge Of The World Sutra. She liked the sound of that. She was a big tea drinker and loved all kinds of tea, especially the deeply moving *puerhs*. She loved reading about tea while drinking tea and reading books about Cha Dao or the Way of Tea. But a tea sutra? Now that was interesting.

She spent some time digging around on the net, which she referred to as "CyberDao" but could find nothing else about it. But instead of becoming discouraged, she felt even more determined to find out more about this strange-sounding sutra.

She asked all her Buddhist-ically minded friends about it but no one had ever heard of such a thing. "Maybe it doesn't really exist," said one of them. "I mean, do you believe everything you see on the internet?"

But Sophie had a feeling, an inkling, an urge, to find out more about this mysterious sutra, which she was sure did exist and also would, hopefully, be a doorway for her to enter a deeper level of practice, both in tea and in meditation, and perhaps even in life itself.

Unfortunately, Sophie did not read Sanskrit or Tibetan and so had to rely upon English translations of various sacred writings, which was not ideal, since many Western scholars knew little about the actual practices of things like meditation and *qigong*, and so their translations were often faulty. She had done enough years of practice to at least know that. But there was often some kernels and nuggets of truth and wisdom, hiding under layers of history and culture in each translation.

She spent a lot of time researching and re-reading and trying to reconstruct whatever clues she could find in the various translations of the various sutras, always hoping they would provide some stepping stones on her journey to find The Teahouse At The Edge Of The World Sutra.

Somehow, she had gotten it into her head and heart that if she could find that elusive, possibly mythical text, that all her years of being a searcher and a seeker would not have been in vain and that she would experience, if not enlightenment, at least some kind of wisdom.

So her search went on. Many times, she was close to giving up, telling herself that it was a stupid quest, as the thing probably did not actually exist. I mean, she would probably have seen some signs of it or at least one of her many teachers may have heard of it themselves. But all of them professed complete ignorance of it. Some of these masters and even lamas were highly erudite and had committed to memory many long sutras and passages of sacred writings, but all of them just shook their heads when she asked them about The Teahouse At The Edge Of The World Sutra.

Actually, when she thought about it, she was not sure where she had even heard about it in the first place. She went through all the books of sacred wisdom that she owned, of which there were many, as well as the usual websites she frequented, but could not find that allusion that she so thought she had seen there. She began doubting herself. Maybe it was a dream, she thought, just a dream. But she had done enough spiritual self-cultivation practice to know that a dream thought was just as real as a so-called waking one, if not more so.

Or maybe is a *terma*, one of those hidden sutras that Padmasambhava, the famous Buddhist hero, hid all over Tibet so that many years later, certain highly evolved aspirants would discover them. Sophie did not consider herself highly evolved, and so perhaps she would never really find this mysterious sutra. But it had gotten a hold on her, and it was increasingly difficult to let go.

One day, after a long afternoon of madly scanning books and websites for new information about the elusive sutra, she found her head falling, slowly but surely, onto her desk in from of her computer. She was out for a few moments but when she came to, she felt a little woozy. Ok, she thought to herself, that's it for today, if not for tomorrow and the day after that. I give up this ridiculous quest for a ridiculous sutra.

She felt she needed some air and perhaps some tea as well. She went to her tea cupboard only to find the cupboard bare and so grabbing her coat, hat, and scarf, made her way down the hill to a cozy teahouse she had occasionally visited.

Every other time she had been there the place had been packed with all kinds of tea loving folks, but today it was totally empty, deserted even. Not only was she the only one there, but there didn't seem to be anyone behind the counter either.

She was not sure if she should stay but decided to sit down at her favorite table and see what happened. She liked this particular table because it was so old and even cracked. Obviously, it had been in use for many years, in the teahouse or perhaps even in someone's home. It reminded her of the great Japanese aesthetic called *wabi sabi*, the appreciation for the old and worn and imperfect. Indeed, she was feeling a bit old and worn and most definitely imperfect these days.

Her eyes were tired from pouring over many books and websites. Her neck hurt from gazing for hours into the computer. Her back was sore from lugging around piles of books from the library to her home. Her heart felt heavy as she realized should probably just give up her dream of finding the sutra and remain unfulfilled, spiritually and emotionally.

Two people came in the door and sat down at her table, right across from her. They did not look familiar, and Sophie wondered why they were sitting down at her very table instead of one of the other empty ones. The two were an old woman and a young man. Though if she blinked, as she tended to do when her eyes were tired, they looked like a young woman and an old man. Blink again and it was an old woman and young man, sitting there across from her, smiling warmly at her, so warmly that she felt a little embarrassed, as if she were meant to recognize them as important people in her life, which she didn't, or at least thought she didn't, though she could not be sure.

Chapter Ten

Suddenly the proprietor of the teahouse appeared at the table. He looked at her only. It was almost as if he did not actually see the other two people at the table, or at least chose to not recognize them as such.

"*Ni hao,*" he said. "*Ni yo bu yo he puerh cha*?" She knew he was speaking Mandarin, of which she only understood a little. She thought he might be asking her if she wanted some tea. So she just nodded yes and said "*hao,*" which she thought might mean yes or good or something like that. He nodded at her and still ignoring the two others at the table, went away to brew her tea.

The two people did not speak to her at first, just smiled their warm smiles, like two cups of warm and lovely tea. She was a little confused and even a bit frightened at first, but then felt herself begin to melt a bit and before long, she was smiling back at them.

"You know," said the young man, "the sutra you seek is not to be found in books or websites."

He looked at the old woman, as if to receive permission to continue. She nodded her head and he went on. "This sutra, The Teahouse At The Edge Of The World Sutra, is what we call a "secret" or "hidden sutra", much like the ones Padmasambhava hid in caves high in the mountains of Tibet. Yes, sometimes they were actually books or texts, but other times they were more like visions. That is what The Teahouse At The Edge Of The World Sutra is. A vision, not a book of any kind. Certainly not a website!" and he laughed, and Sophie found herself laughing right along with him.

Of course, she thought. I should have known.

Then the old woman spoke. She leaned in towards Sophie and put a palm on the middle of Sophie's chest, her heart center. The hand felt light as a feather, but Sophie found herself gasping for a moment, as if there were a great weight on her chest. Then, all of a sudden, the weight was lifted and she felt as light as a feather herself.

"The sutra you seek," said the old woman, "is right here. It has always been here. You have felt it many times when you meditated, when you drank good tea, when you laughed with your friends, when you played with your sister, when you danced in the dark, when you reached out for love, for knowledge, for experience, for healing. It will always be here.

"This kind of sutra," she went on, "is not one that can be written down or imprisoned on a page. It cannot be carried around like furniture. It can only exist in the living heart of the seeker. It can be shared, but only to one who has also realized him or herself as a living embodiment of wisdom; as guide to others who are living in darkness but seeking the light; or as healers in a world that is filled with sickness and ignorance. Indeed, it *must* be shared. If not, it will begin to grow weaker and weaker, like a candle just before the flame goes out.

"Only by sharing this sutra, this vision, will you be able to keep it alive in your heart. Only by sharing what you have learned in your travels, both inner and outer, with others, will the flame of this sutra grow stronger and stronger and never go out. Please remember this."

She lifted her palm then and Sophie felt a great gushing of *qi*, of love, and even of a small part of wisdom, flooding her being. Ah, she thought, ah!

The proprietor of the teahouse appeared at the table once again, carrying a small teapot and one cup, again only looking at her, as if the other two were not there. And, it appeared that her new friends were indeed gone on beyond.

"*Zhe ge hen hao cha,*" he said, smiling at her. Again, she did not know what he was saying, but she understood all the same.

"*Hao,*" she said, "*hen hao,*" and smiling, began drinking her tea.

Chapter Eleven

Dreaming of Tea

Andrew often dreamed of tea, giant cups of it, so big you could swim in it, which he did, as often as he managed to dream it. He had read about something called Lucid Dreaming, where you were supposed to be aware that you were dreaming, and so could fashion the dream however you wanted. That sounded like lots of fun, but he hadn't been able to achieve that, not yet at least, though he hoped that it might just "happen" for him, as apparently it did for others.

But he did dream of tea. His tea dreams were always full of delight. Sometimes there were other people in his dream, people that he was happily drinking tea with. At other times he was alone and his tea drinking then was a little more solemn, though not overly so.

He often drank tea with his friends, fellow tea lovers, many of them much more educated about tea than he was. He had read a few books on tea and on tea ceremony, watched some youtube videos and subscribed to a delightful tea magazine from Taiwan, which had gorgeous photos of tea and teaware and tea ceremony, along with many engrossing articles of tea culture and spirit.

But he felt there was something missing in his tea life, some little thing that might be a key to unlock the door of true tea wisdom. Somehow, it didn't seem that reading books, watching videos and reading tea magazines was quite the key he was looking for. But where could he find it?

Over time, his tea dreams began to get longer and richer. He often found himself sitting by the side of a burbling brook, or a sensuous river, or high in the mountains somewhere in Asia. In his dreams, he often found himself accompanied by other tea dreamers, all interesting and delightful people. They often shared with him important information about tea and even about the very key that he was looking for, but alas, as it often is with dreams, he remembered their words when he first woke up, but by the time he had found some paper and pen, they turned into mere wisps of words and were lost as soon as he tried to write them down.

He tried putting paper and pen right next to his bed, so that he could grab them as soon as he woke up, but they remained wisps and he could not hold them long enough to write them down.

But he was determined to someday remember those wise words of dreams. Each night he went to bed, hoping that this would be the night where what he learned in his dreams could be translated to the world of wakefulness.

One night he had a particularly long and beautiful dream. He was sitting in a teahouse in what seemed like ancient China, though he was not sure just when. He was surrounded by hoards of happy tea drinkers and there seemed to be some sort of storyteller on a small stage at one end of the room. As the storyteller spoke, there were shouts of glee from the tea drinkers, who no doubt, knew the story he was telling by heart already, and were just happy to be caught up in the tale that was told so well.

At first, Andrew felt a little self-conscious, as a 21st century Western guy, but after a while he got so caught up in the story that he forgot all about it. Pretty soon, he realized that he actually understood what the storyteller was saying, and when he looked down, he saw that he was dressed in the same clothing as were all the other ancient Chinese tea drinkers.

So he sat there and smiled to himself. Now this must be the Lucid Dreaming he had read about, he thought to himself. He was able to follow the in's and the out's and the up's and the down's of the story, as though he could speak Chinese, in whatever dialect the storyteller was using. The storyteller was accompanied by a young man who played an *erhu*, an ancient two-stringed, bowed instrument, which in the hands of an artist, could be quite evocative.

Soon he found himself cheering the storyteller on, along with the others in the audience, those fellow Chinese tea drinkers. Funny though, he did not feel Chinese and, even with his Chinese attire, he did not think he would pass as Chinese. Though perhaps he could be wrong, as no one seemed to be staring at him and eventually he began to feel quite at home there in the cheering, shouting, tea drinking audience.

He was suddenly dragged out of his dream by the sound of a car horn blaring outside of his apartment. His neighborhood in London seemed to be full of car horns, a ghastly chorus of them going off all times of night and day. He lay in bed for some time, digesting, remembering, and reimagining his dream. As with most dreams, it had seemed so very real while he was dreaming it. He could still hear the shouts of the crowd and the rising and falling voice of the storyteller.

He went through his day in a bit of a daze, feeling the world shift around him, as he lived his normal day in London, while sometimes seeing, out of the corner of his eye, the teahouse and the storyteller, and even seemed to hear the echoes of the erhu drifting in and out of his consciousness.

He so hoped he would return to the marvelous teahouse in his dreams the next night but alas, he did not. But, after wishing and hoping for a solid week, he found himself back in the teahouse one night.

Again, he was able to understand, not only the storyteller, but all the other patrons. At one point, he was jostled by someone walking by and blurted out "*Dubuqi*" without thinking about it. He knew he was saying, "Excuse me," but he didn't know how he knew it.

The night wore on and many of the patrons had left, until he realized that he was alone, except for the storyteller and his musical accompanist. The musician was placing his instrument into a padded pack and the storyteller was speaking to him in a low tone. Then he suddenly turned to Andrew and said, "*Ni hao wo de pengyou.*" Andrew knew he was greeting him, Andrew, as a friend and he was flattered and flustered.

He did not know what to say and so didn't say anything. The old storyteller spoke again, and though he was speaking Mandarin, Andrew understood everything he said.

"It is nice to see you again. I am glad you seem to enjoy my humble tales, said the storyteller. "*Ni de jia zai nar?*" He asked, "Where is your home?" Meaning, thought Andrew, "where are you from?"

Andrew did not know what to say to this. "I am not from here," he stammered, and the storyteller seemed to know just what he meant.

"I can see that," he said. "You are clearly not of this time or this place. Yet, I believe that in your heart, you have a place and a purpose here."

"I think I may be dreaming right now," Andrew blurted out.

The old storyteller did not seem to be phased by this. "Are we not all dreaming?" he said. "The ancient master Zhuangzi says that we are all dreaming, even though we think we are awake. In our dreaming life we may even try to interpret our dreams! But one day, there will be a Great Awakening and we then will understand that this life that we are so sure is real, is just a dream. And then we will truly awaken."

Andrew did not know what to say to this and so again, said nothing. This seemed to please the old man and he motioned for Andrew

Chapter Eleven

to follow him out of the teahouse. Once they were outside, the air was bracing and the stars above seemed to be hovering right over their heads. Is this how stars look in dreams? thought Andrew. He reached his hand up and it flowed through the stars as if he had put his hand into a stream. A star stream, he thought.

Maybe, he thought, I am not dreaming, and my other life, the one in noisy London, is the real dream. He remembered an old Daoist tale about the man who dreamt he was a butterfly, only to wake up and wonder if, instead of a man who had dreamt he was a butterfly, he was actually a butterfly dreaming he was a man!

The two of them walked silently down a narrow lane that opened up to a broad avenue. Andrew remained silent because he had no idea what to say or what to think about what it was that was happening to him. And the old man seemed to be relishing the silence. Of course, thought Andrew, he has been talking for hours at the teahouse.

They seemed to walk that way for an endless amount of time, but, thought Andrew, "dream time" is very different from "awake time," so who knows how long they really walked? Eventually though, they came to a small building at the end of a very small alley. There was no sign out front and Andrew had no idea what he was getting himself into, but the old man seemed very confident and confidently opened a small door and, ducking his head, entered the building, and Andrew followed.

There was a short hallway of some sort, lighted here and there with twinkling lights. Twinkling lights, thought Andrew, in ancient China. But, as his very British grandfather would say, "In for a penny, in for a pound." He followed the old man down the hallway, which opened up into a small room, with but one table and two chairs. There were no other people about and the old man and Andrew sat down at the table.

The old man smiled at Andrew and said, "I know you are confused right now as to what is real and what is not. All I can say is that "reality" has different layers to it. And each layer is as real as all the others."

As soon as he said this, a pot of tea suddenly appeared on the table, along with two cups of steaming tea. Well this is weird, thought Andrew, but really, no weirder than anything else that's been happening tonight. He lifted one of the cups of tea to his face and inhaled the lovely fragrance. It smelled like his favorite green tea, Dragon Well, though it also had some notes of something else, something old yet fresh, like a really good (and expensive) aged sheng puerh. He tried a small sip and the tea slid down his throat like it was a part of his own body.

He had been so caught up in his own tea journey that he did not notice that the old man had disappeared, and he was alone in the room, in the teahouse. More weirdness.

But to his surprise, Andrew was not concerned and just continued to enjoy his tea. Once his cup was empty, he tried the teapot and to his delight, it was full of more of the delicious tea. So he sat and drank the tea until it the teapot was empty. Then he lifted his head and began to look about him.

The walls of the teahouse if that is what it was, were eight sided, almost round. The ceiling seemed very low and was lined along the edge by more tiny twinkling lights, which were twinkling at him in a friendly way. I like this place, he said to himself. Then he said it out loud, "I like this place."

For whatever reason—the tea, the tiny teahouse, the kind old man, the evening's revelry back at the big teahouse, the blanket of stars that spread under his hand—it all was giving him a feeling of happiness and contentedness. Very different from his usual experience of life as a slog, uphill, in the rain.

I wonder if I am still dreaming, he wondered. He pinched himself and the pinch was indeed painful. He closed his eyes for a moment or two and then opened them and looked around. Still the same tiny teahouse. Still all alone. Still happy.

Andrew began to wonder if indeed, he had ever been happy in his short life. Sure I have been happy, he thought, just not like this. Just not

Chapter Eleven

like now. He wanted the dream, if that is what it was, to go on forever. But he knew, deep down inside his happy heart, that all dreams do come to an end, just as this one would. So what, he thought. So what?

He closed his eyes again for what seemed only a moment, and when he opened them he was walking down the street in London. He saw a small park that he liked and so turned in that direction. In the middle of the park there was an old Chinese man playing the erhu. He was not familiar with that instrument but immediately liked its haunting sound, so he sat down on a bench facing the old man.

The old man was dressed in a modern track suit, grey with blue stripes down the side. He had a long, wispy beard, just like all the old masters Andrew had seen in the *kung fu* movies he so loved.

The soft, soothing sound of the ancient instrument was so peaceful. He sat there for some time, feeling himself relax in places he had been so relaxed in for a long time. The old man seemed lost in his music, though he did once look up and smile at Andrew. It was a funny smile, thought Andrew, almost co-conspiratorial.

That's funny, thought Andrew, and wondered if he and the old man had met before, but he did not think so. Though the longer he sat there, lost in the lovely, shining web of music the old man was weaving, the more he thought maybe he had. Though he had no idea when or where.

He closed his eyes, better to let the music enter his heart. It seemed to only be a moment, but when he opened them again, he was back in the tiny tearoom in the tiny teahouse.

Aha, he thought. Now he was *really* not sure if he were dreaming or awake. But, he thought, does it really matter? Am I the butterfly dreaming of a teahouse or a teahouse dreaming of a butterfly?

He sat there, lost in tea reverie, when suddenly the old man reappeared. He smiled at Andrew and asked if he had enjoyed the tea.

"Very much," said Andrew. "And I love this teahouse, if that is what it is," he said.

"Yes," said the old man, "it is a kind of teahouse, though a very special one. Not many people come here anymore. It seems that the people of today are not really interested in tea magic anymore, but would rather spend time on their computers."

Computers, thought Andrew, are there computers in ancient China? That was when he noticed that the old man was no longer wearing his robe but was wearing a tracksuit. It was grey, with blue lines down the sides. Where had he seen that tracksuit before? he wondered.

He blinked, and there he was in the park in London, enjoying the strange erhu music. He blinked again and there he was in the tiny twinkling teahouse. He tried a few more time-traveling blinks but began to get a little dizzy and had to stop.

The car horn blasted him into "wakefullness." He opened his eyes and looked around. Same old bedroom, in the same old apartment, in the same old Londontown. He closed his eyes and lay there for a while, afraid that if he opened them again, he would find himself back in the twinkling teahouse. Not that he would be upset about that. It was just the rapid movement back and forth in time and space was a bit disorienting.

He thought again about that story of the old Daoist who did not know if he was a man dreaming of his butterfly self or a butterfly dreaming of his human self. Did it really matter? He asked himself once again. Apparently the ancient Daoists did not seem to think so, so really, why should he?

Chapter Eleven

Chapter Twelve

The Boy Who Swallowed The Moon

Once there was a boy named Every. Many people, who being introduced to him, thought his name must be Avery and so called him that. But no, he would say, my name is not Avery, it is Every.

As in everything? they would ask.

Yes, the boy would answer, as in everything. Everything in this world and in any others.

Then he would turn himself away from the questioner and send his attention elsewhere.

Some people would be put off this, thinking it was meant to be a slight. But no, it was just his way of dealing with a world he found difficult to tolerate.

To him, the sound of most people's voices was like the cawing of crows — hard on the ears and upsetting to the soul. His soul anyway.

He was aware that he was different from most people, even his parents, who had birthed him and raised him thus far. But the sound of his own parents was as so much cawing to him. Even the sound of his baby sister, though not as upsetting, was like the sound of a young crow.

He found most of the world very disturbing. And, of course, most people, even his parents, found *him* a bit disturbing.

It was disturbing how he would wince and turn away from them when they tried to speak to him. How he would twitch and shudder when they laid their hands upon him, hoping to sooth his troubled soul.

Some people in the small village, turned away from him and spat on the ground, when he walked by, so that they would not be troubled by the spirit of this troubled boy. Some even called him a devil child.

He spent much, if not most, of his time alone, wandering in the hills around the village. There, people would say, he was communing with evil spirits, if not the devil himself.

Of course, the other children in the village would torment him whenever they came upon him. They pulled his hair, scratched his face, and even threw stones at him. But he would never fight back, never cry, and always took their punishment with saying a word. By and by, the children grew tired and bored with this. After all, it was no fun to torment someone who didn't seem to care what they did. They began to be afraid of him and would run away when they saw him walking back to the village from wherever he had spent the day, alone and out in the lonely hills.

Actually, his parents had not named him Every. They had tried to name him Avery, after his father's father, but the only name he would ever respond to was Every, which is how he heard his name, deep inside himself.

Every was very odd it is true. But also, he was special. Special in the way that a person who has one foot in one world and another in a different world can be. Special in that he experienced the world in a much different way than others did. He saw things and heard things and even felt things that other people did not.

This sometimes caused other people to think that he was dull or stupid or even retarded in some way. But Every was not dull or stupid or retarded in any way. He was just on a different track than other people. Sometimes his track and the world around him would run close together and at other times his track and the world's track, at least the world that his parents and the other villagers were on, veered away sharply.

Every was indeed a very intelligent boy, but intelligent in a different way than most people. Some of the villagers called him "touched," which could mean "not right in the head," or, as in ancient times, touched by the fairy folk or nature beings. (Back when people were intelligent enough to believe in such things.)

Every was indeed touched by these spirit beings, though he perhaps would have not thought of it as such. He did not see himself as remarkable in any way. To him, the world around him seemed very strange and even crazy at times, while he himself was often the only "sane" person he knew.

He knew of course, that he was seen as different by the others in the village, even scary or dangerous. But he knew that it was *their* problem, not his. All he tried to do each day of his life was keep out of everyone else's way and go his own. If others felt strange or threated by that, there was really nothing he could do about it.

One day, deep in his ramblings, he came upon a cave. The opening was hidden by some large bushes, which is why, although had passed that way a hundred times, he had never noticed the cave before. He approached it slowly; in case it was the home of a large animal.

Every loved animals and spent as much time as he could with them. He had learned how to call the birds, in a language they understood. They would come and perch on his shoulders and peck gently at his earlobes. He could also call rabbits and deer and all kinds of other animals, each in their own language, which he had, somehow, taught himself. Oftentimes when he appeared to others as talking to himself, another sign of his being "touched," he was actually teaching himself animal languages. He didn't really know how he did this; it was just enough for him that he did.

But he had never learned bear language and he was a little afraid of them, truth be told. He certainly did not want to wake up a slumbering, grouchy bear!

He approached the cave very slowly and cautiously. But once he was able to poke his head into the cave, he saw that it was empty. It did not smell like an animal. It did not smell musty or dangerous. It smelled good — like herbs, like flowers, like tea.

Every enjoyed drinking tea with his mother, and sometimes with his father, when his father was not too busy with farm work. They would sit in front of the fire pit and drink the tea slowly, letting all the good flavors of the tea enter their heart and body. Of course, Every would not talk to his parents at this time. He hardly ever spoke to them. They often saw him talking to himself, very seriously, in some weird, made-up language, but no one ever realized that he was speaking in different animal tongues.

But he did enjoy sitting in silence with these two strange (to him) people that had borne him and fed him and looked after him all through his infancy and even now, provided food and bed and a cozy hut, even though he spent little time there.

He would gaze deeply into his teacup and often saw strange shapes of strange beings and strange places, though he, of course, never shared that with his parents. And they, in turn, would just sit and look at their strange son and enjoy spending time with him, even in this way.

As Every moved further into the cave, he saw that it was much, much deeper than he had at first thought. He kept moving deeper and deeper, listening and watching intently, on the lookout for an angry bear.

But there was no angry or otherwise bear there. He just kept moving futher and further into the cave and the warm smell of herbs and flowers and tea began to get stronger.

As he got deeper into the cave, it of course, got darker. But then, it seemed that the further and deeper he got into the cave, the lighter and brighter it became. Suddenly, he came out into a large room, which was very bright and smelled very good.

He saw that there was a girl about his own age, sitting in front of a fire pit with a large kettle of water that hung from the tripod above the flames, which was bubbling and hissing along. Every looked at the pot and heard its song and smelled the good smell of herbs and flowers and tea.

The girl smiled at him and motioned for him to join her around the fire. So Every slowly made his way over to her and sat himself down, right across from her. The girl smiled and he found himself smiling back, which was a bit disconcerting to him. But he just could not help himself, she was smiling so brightly, like a sun in a blue sky.

Presently, the girl took a large ladle and took out some the dancing water and poured it into a large clay bowl, all the while smiling and nodding to Every, though without speaking. Then she held up a smaller clay bowl, filled with herbs. She passed it over to Every so that he could be introduced to them. Every looked at them and smelled them, recognizing them as some kind of tea.

It smelled like the forest and the creek that run through the middle of it and the flowers that grew alongside the creek and even the smell of the forest animals that drank from the creek. It smelled like the rain, when it was falling very softly in the spring, and of the wind that blew ever so gently then, and of the earth that breathed beneath his feet wherever he walked and the sky that smiled down on him as he moved through the world.

He passed it back to the girl, who received it as if he were offering her a great gift. She picked up a clay teapot and dropped a great handful of the tea into it and then filled that with the dancing water. Then she sat back and smiled again at Every, who was sitting across from her and watching her through the flames that danced between them.

Even though she did not speak out loud, Every heard every word she spoke to him. He heard it as a song, a song much like the ones his bird friends would sing to him and like the ones he sang back to them. He heard it like the creek running joyfully through the forest and he heard it like the sun that smiled down on him as he lay back on the soft grass beside the creek. And he heard it like the earth that sang beneath him as lay there, snug in his own body, at home in the forest as he never felt at home in his own home.

The girl, still silently singing, poured some of the tea into a large clay cup, much larger than the ones his parents used, and passed it through the flames to him. He held it gently in his cupped hands, like the way he would hold the tiny birds that came to him when he sang their song.

It was so large and a bit heavy and very hot, yet Every held it tightly but loosely, like a living breathing creature.

The girl smiled at him again but now she seemed to be getting lighter and lighter, and harder to see, and then he could see her no more, as she floated up to the ceiling of the cave, like a puff of smoke.

Every was sorry to see her go but he still felt happy there in front of the fire, with his large bowl of tea in his gently cupped hands.

He looked down into his cup and he saw there, not the reflection of the ceiling of the cave but sky outside the cave. He saw the stars there, twinkling in their own language, (one that he was still learning) and he saw the moon there, riding high in the sky like a ship on a vast sea.

He smiled into the cup and the moon smiled back, not asking for anything in return, not wanting him to be anything than what he was. She smiled at him and sang to him in her own lovely moon language. He sang back to her, very softly, in his own very own Every language, the one he only sang to himself when he was alone.

He smiled at her with a smile as big as the sky and then, lifting the cup to his lips, drank down the moon.

Chapter Thirteen

The Man Who Knew Too Much
A Story of Enlightenment and Tea

There was once a great Master who had studied all the esoteric knowledge and all the spiritual teachings of all the great masters. He had traveled for many years all around the world, studying with this master and that. He had read all the great books that had been written and had spent years in deep meditation high in the mountains of the Himalayas. He had practiced secret tantric rites, both with a female consort and with the bones of ancient masters. He had reflected on himself as a numinous being as well as a bony skull, waiting for death for release from the material world. He himself had written many dense and obtuse works of spiritual knowledge. He had taught at many of the great universities as well as the great spiritual centers around the world. He had many students, some of whom would have worshiped him if he had allowed it.

He had many lovers and had fathered numerous children, all of whom, he had announced, would grow up to be sages. He had looked death in the face and laughed. He had spent vast sums of money, most of it donated to him by his many wealthy students, building grand temples and ashrams but never stayed at one of them for long, for he was a restless spirit and was always drawn on to the next new teacher, the next new lover, the next new spiritual experience.

He could control his body temperature and had studied *tumo* with Tibetan monks and could dry a dozen wet sheets wrapped around him as he sat by a freezing lake high in the Himalayas. He had meditated with Shiva-worshipping sadhus in India and had smoked vast quantities of hashish with them as they sat meditating by the burning ghats along the sacred Ganges. He had watched many people's bodies transform from human beings to piles of glowing ash.

He was famous and rich and very, very successful and many called him enlightened, but he was not satisfied. He was restless but could not say what it was he was restless about. He felt he was missing out on something very important and perhaps even crucial, but he could not say what that very important and crucial thing was. All he knew was that he did not have it and he felt he would never be whole until he did.

He stopped traveling, stopped public speaking and writing, and shut himself deep within his meditation chamber. He refused food and drank only a small amount of fruit juice a day, just enough to keep himself alive while he went deep inside himself to find what it was that he was missing.

But, after many days of this he felt no closer to the elusive something than when he had started, and he became very angry. Then he became very depressed. He sat listlessly in his room, deep in the heart of his ashram and looked idly out the window and sighed deep, sad sighs.

Then one day one of his students begged for an audience with him, saying that he had made a great discovery and wanted to share it with his guru. The great Master decided that he was so completely bored that he would speak with someone, even if it was a student, and a not very advanced one either.

When the student came into his presence, and after making obeisance to him, told him that he had found a great teacher, one who far surpassed all other teachers, one who was as the sun to the moon, as a shining lotus flower to a weed, whose immense knowledge dwarfed all other spiritual teachers.

The Master began, in spite of himself, to become interested. He was sure that he had already met all the great masters of the age and had gleaned from them whatever knowledge they possessed. But perhaps there was still yet one whom he had not met and who might have an answer to his problem.

He was becoming interested. His student then told him where this great teacher could be found. It was in a little tea shop, which was located in a run-down part of the city, upstairs from a laundry. This does not sound promising, said the great Master to himself, but he decided he would go there anyway and see if there was not some crumb of knowledge he could glean from this teacher.

After consulting his star chart and other divinatory tools for an auspicious day, he followed his student's directions and traveled to a part of the city where he had never been before. As he picked his way through the congested streets, he found himself becoming more and more convinced that he was wasting his time. How could there be any sort of realized master in this part of town? he thought to himself. He knew that great masters always dwelt in the mountains where they could breathe the pure air and be closer to the spiritual realm, or else deep within sacred caves where they would not be polluted by the dust of the world, or else in ashrams or temples, where they would be closer to the divine energy of the gods.

And so, as he picked his way through the mounds of trash and dog feces (he was, as usual, wearing sandals, which had cost a lot of money, and which he did not want to be smeared with dog feces) he began to have greater and greater doubts. But he decided to go on and see it through to the end. After all, if he could spend all that time in the

Himalayas studying arcane tantric arts and smoke all that pungent and incredibly potent hashish with the sadhus while they watched the fat bubble on the bodies of the dead, he figured he could handle traveling through these nasty streets.

After some time, he came to the laundry, from which clouds of odiferous steam emerged and, after poking around for some time, found a set of dilapidated steps leading up to the second floor. He climbed up the stairs, which squeaked and squawked under his feet and threatened to crumble before his weight with every step, until he found himself at the door to the teashop. Not that there was any written sign there indicating there was a business there, but there was a crude picture of a tea pot with steam rising out of its spout in the shape of a dragon, so he figured he was in the right place.

He tried knocking a few times but when that got no response, he tried the door and, finding it unlocked, he opened it and entered the tiny and cluttered shop. No one was about and he spent a few minutes surveying the room. It was indeed very small and was filled with shelf after shelf of various clay jars of tea. There were also many clay teapots, some of them fantastically shaped and most of them covered in a thin film of dust.

He looked around some more until he found a small table with several tiny stools in front of it, the very low stools like the ones used by the peasants in China. He wondered where the proprietor could be and was on the point of leaving when suddenly a door he had not noticed before opened at the back of the room, and a very old and very odd-looking man came through. He was so bent over that his head was aligned with his waist and he needed to look up and twist his neck around so that he could see his visitor.

"Ah," he said, with a great smile, which seemed to emerge from out of his wrinkled face like the sun coming out of a cloud. "I did not know I had a customer. Please forgive my inattentiveness. I'm afraid I have no excuse." He tried to bow a little lower, but he was already so

Chapter Thirteen

hunched over that to bow any further was impossible.

The Master was feeling a bit uncomfortable and would have liked to have left but the little man was smiling so sweetly at him that he decided it would have been very rude and so he decided to take a few moments to be cordial to this funny looking old man and then be on his way.

The old man pointed to one of the tiny stools and invited the Master to sit. The stool looked so small and old and fragile that the Master was very sure it would not support his weight but, in the interest of politeness, he decided to try it. As he lowered himself onto the stool, he was surprised to find it held up very well. He relaxed then and breathed out a deep sigh. For some strange reason this miniature stool felt more comfortable than the throne he usually sat upon when receiving pilgrims at the ashram.

The old man smiled again at him and said, in a very loud voice, "Please wait a moment, good sir, while I make us some tea."

The Master began to protest that this was not needed but cut himself off. Perhaps it would be nice to have a hot cup of tea before he left, he thought to himself. He sat and watched as the old man shuffled around the room in an odd fashion that looked as though he were floating a little above the floor.

"I have some very good *Lung Jing*, Dragon Well, tea here from a friend who lives in Hangzhou," he said, in that loud voice. "I just can't exactly remember what I did with it," he said, while searching through the many jars that sat upon the shelves. "Ah," he said at last, "here it is." He shuffled on over to the table where the Master sat and plopped himself down on the stool opposite him. "Now we shall drink some tea and become acquainted." Here he looked over expectantly at the Master, who looked back at him, feeling more curious by the moment about just who this old man was.

Suddenly the old man started. "Oh dear," he said, "I forgot to get the water!" And here he jumped up and shuffled across the room again in his funny floating way and disappeared behind the door from which he had emerged earlier. In just a moment he was back again, carrying a steaming kettle of hot water. "I had just put it on right before you arrived," he said. "I have been *so* looking forward to this meeting."

The Master wondered to himself how in the world the old man had known of his visit before he had arrived but decided that his student had probably told him. For some reason he felt very relaxed there, sitting on the ridiculously small stool looking over as the old man placed a small handful of tea leaves into a small clay teapot. This Dragon Well tea, the Master knew, was a favorite of poets and artists. He watched as the old man then poured the water onto the leaves and then put the lid onto the pot.

"We must wait for a moment or two while the water and the leaves dance together," said the old man, looking over at the Master with such a sweet and accepting gaze that he felt a little flushed. He was used to people looking at him in awe and even worshipfully, but this was different. The old man looked over at him in complete acceptance he felt, not because of who he was or what his attainments were but just as a fellow traveler on the road of life.

Yet it was more than that. It was as if the old man could see right down deep into his heart and, upon seeing the real essence of his being, not only accepted him but even *approved* of him. Again, he had the feeling that to the old man he was not the great Master that most people saw, but just a fellow human being and worthy to be accepted and treated with warmth and friendship.

The Master felt something stir within him as he sat there. Perhaps this old man truly *was* a great teacher. Perhaps he had the answer to the question that had plagued him these last few years. He wanted to speak up right then and there but, for some reason, felt shy about doing so. This is odd, he thought to himself, he had never felt this sense of shyness with anyone before, not even the Dalai Lama or any of the other great teachers and masters he had met. He decided to hold his tongue for the moment and see what the old man said.

The old man suddenly reached over to the teapot and began pouring the steaming liquid into two round clay cups. "I find that when I get anxious or stressed all it takes is a good cup of tea to make things right again. That is," and here he looked over at the Master with a quick and penetrating gaze, "if I truly relax and allow the tea to do its work on my soul."

Now that is an odd thing to say about a cup of tea, thought the Master to himself. He reached over and picked up his cup and made to drink it. "Wait," said the old man. "We must first inhale the rich aroma of the tea and let it make its way down into our bodies and souls."

There was that strange phrase again, thought the Master, as if tea could have an effect on our souls. But he dutifully took up his cup and held it before his nose and inhaled deeply. Yes, he thought, this is good tea. The aroma seemed to enter his nose and reach down into his heart. He felt something unclench there. What was that? he thought.

"Now we drink," said the old man and lifted the cup to his lips and drank. The Master did the same. It was strange but as the tea entered his mouth, he felt his whole being stretch forward to receive it. I wonder if the old man has bewitched this tea, he thought to himself and felt a short pang of fear but, just as quickly, he put that thought out of his mind and just allowed the sweet goodness of the tea to enter his being. He felt himself relaxing in a way he hadn't for some time.

The old man was looking at him over the rim of his cup. While it was true he was still terribly bent over, at the same time it looked as though he was sitting straight and tall and looking over at the Master on an equal level. The Master shook his head and again the old man was bent over and drinking his cup of tea with both hands.

"You know," said the old man, "tea once saved my life."

At this the Master looked up expectantly. He wondered how this could be so. He had always loved a good story and so he looked forward to this one.

"It was during the so-called Great Proletariat Cultural Revolution," the old man said. "Such a dark time." Here he stopped and took another sip of this tea. His body was so bent over that he seemed to be having some trouble swallowing. But after a moment he went on. "The Red Guards had come to my hometown and set about destroying the Four Old's. They were children really, so young. Yet they were willful and destructive children, and they were on a mission to destroy the old traditions and had the blessing of the Great Helmsman.

"They had already smashed everything in the local temple and had beaten the few priests that had not run off. They had made a huge bonfire of all the paintings and books that they had torn out of the temple and the villagers' homes. Some of these had been in families for generations. People were crying but the Red Guards only beat them when they tried to resist or even when they expressed their emotions about what was happening.

"I stood on the edge of the crowd. I had no belongings that interested the Red Guards. Or at least not at first. But after looking through my house the first time and not finding anything of value there they decided to look a little closer. I had, of course, hidden anything of value out back in the privy before they came."

"How did you know they were coming?" asked the Master.

"Oh," said the old man, "the tea told me. Just as it did about you."

The Master was not sure he had heard right. "Does the tea speak to you then?" he asked.

"Oh yes," replied the old man. "It always has." He cleared his throat and went on. "The second time they came through they found a small teapot that had been in my family for seven generations. It was such a small and ugly thing that I had not thought to hide it. But, as it was obviously old, even ancient, it was a great find for the Red Guard.

"'What is this?' they shouted, spitting in my face in their excitement. "This looks like contraband from the Imperial Feudal times. You should have turned this in the first time we came here. But instead, you sought to hide it from us,' which was ridiculous since it sat right up on a shelf in plain sight. But they were rapturous at their find. I could see that, in their excitement they meant to use me as an example. They raged all around my small house, ripping shelves down and destroying all my pitiful furniture. Meanwhile several of them guarded me, lest I escape.

"When they were done, they held up the very small, old and very ugly tea pot in my face and shouted 'Why do you hide this old feudal thing from us? Why did you not destroy this as you were supposed to?' They actually spat in my face they were so excited. So I said the first thing that popped into my head. 'Because its magic!' I shouted.

"This stopped them in their tracks. Because you know, even if a few of them were from the city, most of the Red Guards were country boys and girls. They did not have the sophistication of their fellows from the big city.

"I looked at them and saw so many emotions playing across their faces. The city ones were, of course, contemptuous, but I could see that the country ones believed, almost against their will, a little of what I had said.

"'What do you mean, magic,' they thundered and threw me to the floor. 'There is no such thing in modern China!' They kicked me then and would have done much worse, but I could see that a few of them wanted to know more about what I was saying. 'Show us this magic,' they shouted, shoving the teapot into my face.

"I wasn't sure what to do. So, I gingerly reached out for the teapot and got up from the floor. 'I need to heat some water,' I said, so you can see the magic.' When they allowed me to rise and hobble over to the stove, I knew I had them. The ones from the city were, of course, sneering at me, but the country ones, while they also tried to sneer, looked at me as if I might decide to sprout wings and fly away. Many of them had grown up around priests and shamans and some part of them still believed in the old ways, even if they were not supposed to.

"I heated water for the tea. I had some *Lung Ching* tea left, the same kind we are drinking now. I brought the water to a boil and then let it sit a moment. 'What are you doing?' shouted the Red Guards, especially the city ones. 'I am waiting for the water to transform,' I told them. This caused much muttering, and I could see the city ones were going to lose their patience soon if I did not produce something good.

"After waiting a few moments, I began to pour the water into the teapot, which I had filled with a huge handful of tea leaves. In reality, it only takes a small amount of high-quality tea leaves to brew good tea but I wasn't going to take any chances. After I poured the water, I set the teapot on the counter and walked over to the other side of the room. 'What are you doing?' they shouted. 'I am now waiting for the marriage of the tea and water to finish. Then you will see some magic.'

"Of course, this made them all very upset. The city ones were running out of patience with me, and I could see the violence in their eyes. But the country ones wanted to make sure. 'Hold on,' they said to the others. 'He is just a stupid old man and when we see that he has no magic we will beat him and break his ugly old teapot.'

"This seemed to calm the city ones down a bit, and they smiled in anticipation of the good beating they were going to give me. After a few more minutes I went over to the teapot, which now held a strong brew of tea. 'You have broken all my cups,' I said to them. 'We will have to drink out of the pot itself.' I knew that many country people did not use teacups but just drank straight out of the teapot, so the country ones did not think that strange.

"'I will drink first,' I said and raised the teapot to my mouth. They all stood around me then, their muscles tense, as if they were getting ready to flee at a moment's notice. I took a small sip and shouted, 'Long life to Chairman Mao!' Of course, they all had to shout along with me. I took another small sip and shouted, 'Ten Thousand Years for

Chairman Mao!' I knew I was taking a chance with this one. The phrase Ten Thousand Years was what they used to say to the emperor! But I was counting on the fact that, even though Mao was not in name, the emperor, to these youngsters he might as well have called himself that, so exalted was he to them.

"So, I decided to go out on a limb. 'I now call upon all the spirits of this village to enter this teapot in the name of the great Chairman Mao!' I held the teapot over my head and shook it a bit, as if unseen beings were entering it. Then I lowered it and offered it to the Red Guards. 'Please drink to Chairman Mao,' I said to them. One by one they came forward to drink from the pot. Of course, once I had dedicated it to their great leader, they would not dare to turn me down. One by one they came forward and drank from the teapot.

"What they were not prepared for was the electric tingle of the tea as it entered their mouths. I could see each one of them jump as they tasted it. I could see that the country ones were sure that spirits had entered it. Even some of the city ones, I could see, were convinced that *something* had altered the tea. Of course, what they did not know, and would never know if I could help it, was that, in addition to the great amount of tea I had filled the teapot with, I had also surreptitiously dumped a good amount of red pepper powder into it. The strong spice had been left on the counter from the night before when I had used it to make my favorite Szechwan dish, *Kung Pao Dofu*.

"Once the teapot was emptied, they acted very differently than before. They offered the teapot back to me, almost shyly. A few of them even bowed to me. The city ones were still a little unconvinced and said to me "Remember next time, old man, not to try and trick us. We will not be so lenient with you then!'

"I smiled and bowed to them, holding the teapot to my chest. The pain in my back from when they had thrown me to the floor, was already beginning to travel up my spine, but I held back my tears and smiled at them. 'Love live Chairman Mao,' I called to them, brandishing the teapot.

"After they finally left, I collapsed to the floor, the pain in my back so strong I wept aloud with it. Later on, one of my neighbors came by to check up on me and found me there on the floor and helped me to my bed. I was babbling by this time. 'It was the pepper,' I kept saying, 'it was just the pepper.'

'What are you talking about?' asked my neighbor. I tried to tell her about tricking the Red Guards but I'm afraid I made very little sense. Finally, I blurted out, 'In the teapot, look and see.' So she went over to the counter where I had laid the teapot before I collapsed to the floor. She opened the top and smelled it. She looked at me curiously. Finally, she upended the pot and shook out the last few drops of tea there. 'This tea tastes fine," she said, 'it is a little strong, but it is good Dragon Well.'

"'Bring it here,' I said, and she dutifully brought it over to me. I opened the lid myself and smelled. It smelled like tea and nothing else. I cautiously dipped my finger into the mass of damp tealeaves and brought it to my lips. Nothing but the taste of tea. But what had happened to the pepper that I was been sure I put into it?

"'On the counter,' I said, 'red pepper.' My neighbor went to the counter and looked around. 'Things are a bit of a mess here,' she said, shaking her head. 'But there is no red pepper, only the dust from the bottom of the tea canister.'

"How could this be true? I asked myself. I was sure I had put red pepper in the teapot, not tea dust. What had made the tea so hot and spicy I wondered. Could it really have been the local spirits entering it? Whatever it was, I thought, it had saved my life. Yes, I was in pain and the injury did leave me as you see me now but if I had been wrong and the tea had not worked its miracle on the ferocious Red Guards, they would have surely killed me."

The tea in their cups was gone now and the old man filled the teapot with hot water once again. The Master sat there wondering what to say. He had heard more amazing stories than this one on his travels around the world but, for some reason, he felt very touched by this one. Maybe it was the sweet smile of the old man who, after having suffered so much, seemed to be happy and content here in his tiny shop.

Perhaps, he thought to himself, he is the teacher that I have been searching for. He decided to tell the old man who he was and what his accomplishments were. He would list for him the various initiations he had gone through, what spiritual powers he had attained, what masters he had already studied with in these long years, how many people he had already touched with his spiritual force, how many people he had healed, how famous he was. He knew, of course, that he was bragging but it seemed important to him to establish himself in the old man's eyes before the old man might impart something of his vast wisdom to him.

He began to speak, but just as he did the old man got up and came over to the Master's side of the table. "Allow me to fill your cup," he said, warmly. He tipped the pot of hot tea into the Master's cup. On and on he went until it began to spill over and run all over the table. Surely, he sees what he is doing," thought the Master. He was about to say something as the old man continued to pour and pour hot tea until it ran over the edge of the table onto his lap!

He leapt up, his thighs having been scalded with the hot tea and sputtered, "Do you not see what you are doing old man? You have poured hot tea all over my lap!"

The old man then stopped pouring the tea and looked up at the Master with a gentle smile. "I know very well what I have done," he said. "Your mind and heart are so full of your past accomplishments my friend that I am afraid, just as with this cup, there is no room for me to fit anything else into it."

The Master wobbled a little and sank suddenly back down onto the tiny stool. He felt something move within him and he was flooded with tears. It was true, he *was* already filled to the brim. How could anyone reach him, the way he was? He remembered something he had read long ago from the *Dao De Jing*, the sacred book of the Daoists.

> In the world of knowledge,
> Every day something is added.
> In the world of Dao,
> Everyday something is let go.

He lowered his head and bowed to the old man. He bowed so low that his head was actually lower than that of the bent old man. "Teacher," he exclaimed. "You are right. Please enlighten me!"

The old man continued to sit there and smile at the Master. The Master felt something vast moving in his being and he began to weep. And as he did so, he felt all the accumulation of his spiritual quest pour out of him along with his tears. He sat and wept for a long time, so great were his accumulations. When at last he felt empty he lifted his head to the old man.

"Please," he said, as he held out his teacup. "May I have some more tea?"

It is said that this man, who knew too much, spent much of his time visiting the old tea master and drinking many kinds of tea with him. They spoke of this and that and the old man never seemed to be sharing anything special but when the Master returned home, he always felt refreshed and full of joy.

On that first visit to the tea master, as he he was leaving to go down the stairs to the street, he noticed a small sign that he had missed before. In archaic characters, which the Master could, of course read, being the highly educated man he was, it said, The Teahouse At The Edge Of The World.

Chapter Fourteen
Robot Tea

The 999 version of the Robot Tea Server had just come out and Wanda was very excited. No longer would she have to rely on human tea servers, which were becoming hard to find, and once found, hard to rely on, for various reasons. Sometimes they would show up late or not at all. Sometimes they would pick the wrong tea (a big faux pas in Wanda's opinion). Or they would put out too many cups or not enough, another big one.

Or they would fumble the teakettle and burn themselves, or even worse, one of the clients. Or they would engage in too much small talk. Wanda hated that. She wanted all her tea clients to be having a really Zen time and not engaging too much with each other or the tea master.

Or, the worst, they would have their own opinion about certain teas and how to prepare and serve it. All in all, Wanda wanted them to just do what she told them to do, no more and certainly no less. Basically, she wanted a tea server with little to no personality to get in the way of the Zen experience of her customers.

Which is why she was so excited about the new Robot Server 999. She could program it to exactly the specifications that she wanted. Of course, it could also serve as a bartender or even a waiter but what Wanda wanted and what Wanda was going to be sure to get, is just the perfect tea server, one with no personality and no problems.

Of course, some people actually preferred a human tea server. Those traditionalists, who still clung to the old, outmoded style of tea ceremony. Wanda had no patience for those types. They could just stay in their Stone Age traditions of tea. Wanda was firmly on the newer path of personality-less tea serving. The old-fashioned tea ceremony was too much for her. Who wanted to spend time reciting poetry and slowly enjoying the flavor and texture and spiritual aspects of tea? Not Wanda.

The new thing about tea ceremony was to just sit, quietly and humbly, and to be served by a tea robot with no muss and no fuss. Sure, it was fun to learn about new teas, but that was all in the brochure that people got when they signed up for one of Wanda's tea ceremonies.

Yes, tea could be a philosophical and even spiritual path, but that is not what *she* focused on. *Her* focus was to get some expensive tea into people and get them out so she could get some more clients in to drink and buy some more expensive tea.

Wanda had no patience for the old-fashioned Cha Dao people, who she considered totally out of touch with modern times and boring to boot. Yet she had named her teahouse the very exotic and somewhat mysterious name of The Teahouse At The Edge Of The World. Just enough exoticism and mysteriousness that would make her clients feel like they were visiting an old style teahouse, though of course everything was very modern and up to date. Not to mention that old style teahouses were becoming very rare indeed.

So when the day came for her delivery of her Robot Tea Server 999, she was very excited. Sure enough, it appeared on her doorstep on the appointed day, and she quickly dragged it into her tea business cubicle. When she opened the box and took it out, the Robot Tea Server 999 looked a little small for the job. But when she read the directions, it seemed that it would be able to fill her needs quite well.

There was a panel that opened in the back with all kinds of knobs and dials that she needed to push and turn in the right direction to program it correctly. Wanda was a little uncomfortable doing this, as she was not technically inclined, but she spent quite a bit of time to get it right. Hopefully.

When she turned it on, the Robot Tea Server 999's eyes lit up in a very pleasant way but made no sound, which made Wanda happy. She did not like the idea of it making all kinds of robot noises to spoil the Zen experience of her well-heeled clients.

She placed it behind the tea table, which was encrusted with various crystals and magical symbols, most of which she had knew nothing about. She just knew that her clients liked them, imagining that they somehow made the tea ceremony more magical and special, as they imagined themselves to be.

She picked out some tea from her shelf, not the most expensive, but still good stuff. She filled the teakettle and turned the dial that said "fisheyes," and then sat back and let the Robot Tea Server 999 do its thing.

For a moment or so the Robot Tea Server 999 just sat there, emitting no sounds, and doing nothing. Then it seemed to suddenly wake up and turned to the gently steaming teakettle. And after a few moments, when the teakettle was at full boil, it gently lifted it and poured it into a small teapot that sat before it, making sure to shower the teapot with hot water after it did so.

Wanda had put two tiny teacups on the table and the Robot Tea Server 999 poured the hot water from the teapot into each one, warming them up to just the right temperature. So far, so good.

Wanda had chosen a slightly aged sheng puerh, not the *most* aged and certainly not the most expensive. That was for her high roller tea clients, the ones who were not afraid to drop a thousand or more or more on a small cake of really aged tea.

The Robot Tea Server 999 was giving off the faintest whirring sound, but Wanda did not seem to mind it. It actually was kind of comforting. The Robot Tea Server 999 poured out the hot water in each cup and then filled the little teapot with the (very expensive) tea and poured hot water for the first steeping. Wanda had been a little unsure if she wanted the first steeping to be poured off or keep it. The teacake was not super tight but she decided to have it poured it off and so had programmed the robot to do so.

The Robot Tea Server 999 then poured hot water into the teapot and waited the appropriate time to pour it off. Of course, different tea manuals suggested slightly different times to steep the tea but Wanda decided to go with one of the preprogramed times available to the robot and so had programmed it accordingly.

After the programmed time, the robot poured out the tea into a slightly bigger pot and then into the two cups. It then sat back, and the whirring stopped and the light that was in place of its eyes, which was probably just a feature to make it seem more alive, blinked off.

Wanda took a sip of the tea. It was good, not too strong, not too weak, or insipid. Wanda hated insipid tea and she imagined that most of her wealthy clients felt the same.

All in all, it seemed that the inaugural session with the Robot Tea Server 999 had gone very well. Wanda picked up her phone and sent out a text to some of her wealthier clients and invited them to a special tea session, featuring some 1940's sheng that she was sure they would be drooling over.

The next evening, several high roller clients entered the tea space. The lighting was muted, only the sounds of the special *feng shui* music program was issuing out of Wanda's computer, which was tucked away behind a large *Enso* or Zen circle, one that had been done by a computer of course. Humans were never able to draw the perfect circle that a computer could.

Wanda took out the remote and turned on the Robot Tea Server 999. It's robot eyes lit up and the faint whirring sound began. Everyone at the tea table oo'd and ah'd. Wanda allowed herself one small smile.

This was *just* the response she had hoped for.

She leaned across the table and took out the cake of 40's sheng pu-erh she intended to serve and sell this night. Passing it around so that her clients could smell its wonderfully aged and earthy smell brought more oo's and ah's.

The tea smelled of trees, of earth, of sky, of rain and the wonderful woody smell of the warehouse it had been stored in for so long. Of course, Wanda kept all her special and expensive teas in a climate-controlled storeroom, but this tea still retained the deep and somewhat ancient feeling of a tea that had been grown and produced so many years ago. Long, long before this present moment, in which they would get to experience for themselves what it was like to drink such an aged (and expensive) tea. She could see that her clients were very excited about the whole thing — the age of the tea, the lovely surroundings of the teahouse and the tantalizing idea of being served by one of the first robot tea servers.

At first all went well. The Robot Tea Server 999 checked the temperature of the quietly bubbling, "fisheyes" water. It then filled the teapot with the water and poured it out. But then, instead of filling the pot with tea, the robot dumped the tea onto the table beside the teapot. Then it dumped the hot water onto the floor.

The clients were becoming a bit confused and disconcerted. What was happening here? Was all this some kind of charade or was there some deeper meaning in the robot's movements?

Meanwhile, Wanda was madly pushing buttons on the remote, all to no avail. The Robot Tea Server 999 turned to the clients and the whirring sound became louder and the eerie, lit-up eyes seemed to get brighter and brighter. It was almost as if the robot were laughing at them.

They all turned to Wanda, who shrugged. I am fucked, she thought, royally fucked.

Then the robot picked up the cake of the ridiculously expensive cake and threw it at the wall, where it shattered into many pieces, some even falling into the laps of the totally confused clients.

Fucked, fucked, fucked, said Wanda to herself, over and over.

Then something strange and wonderful happened. One of the clients, the oldest one, and possibly the only one who remembered what tea ceremonies had been like "in olden times," picked up the shard of sheng that had landed in his lap and smiled a big wide smile. He lifted the tea to his nose and inhaled deeply.

"I see," he said. "The robot is teaching us that it is our attachment to the form of the tea and the tea ceremony that is limiting us in our experience and appreciation of the tea and this endless moment."

The other clients started nodding their heads. Surely this is what was going on, they all agreed. "The robot is leading us from a state of what we think we know about tea and tea ceremony," he continued, "and liberating us from our small and insipid understanding and opening us to something greater and vaster."

At this point the robot started pointing with its stubby fingers at each of the clients in turn. As it did so, each client, in turn, bowed deeply to the robot. Wonderful they thought, just wonderful.

While this was happening, Wanda had gone from "I'm completely fucked" to "wow, maybe this will turn out ok," though she was still surreptitiously punching buttons on the remote, to no avail.

The robot then turned to Wanda and pointed at her. She felt herself bowing back, before she was even aware of it. Then the robot emitted a strange sound from deep in its entrails. It sounded almost like a chuckle, if such a thing were possible from a robot. Then it suddenly shut down, its lighted eyes dimming to nothing.

Everyone sat there for a few moments, and then the clients began to applaud, laughing quietly to themselves.

After they all had left, each with a small part of the ancient cake in their hands, expertly wrapped up in translucent rice paper by Wanda, she sat in the teahouse, still wondering what the hell had just happened.

Chapter Fifteen

The Teahouse for Ghosts
Part Two

Once in a while, people find themselves at the ghost teahouse, even though they are not technically ghosts. Meaning they have not actually died, but are in some kind of limbo, in between place.

This is, of course, very confusing for these people. They find themselves surrounded by ghosts, who are all very curious about them. The ghosts are a bit insubstantial, while the people are very substantial, solid even.

"How did I get here?" ask the people, who stand, surrounded by a sea of ghosts. "I am not dead," they say to the ghostly figures floating around them. "At least I don't think I am."

Then they start to think, "Maybe I am. Perhaps I am dead and don't realize it. Though I certainly do not remember dying."

"Maybe I died in my sleep," they wonder. But when they see how insubstantial the ghosts are and how very substantial, they are, they start to doubt again.

Finally, they get upset and shout, "I am not dead, and I am certainly not a ghost. What in the world (or beyond it) am I doing here?"

This is when the bodhisattva ghosts who run the teahouse come out, tea towel over their arms and smiles on their ghostly faces.

"*Mei wen ti*. No problem," they say, "no problem." Though their smiles look a little half-hearted and their voices are hard to hear, what with all the many ghosts all floating around the place, all talking at once.

"I am sure it is just a little mix-up," they say, and attempt to put a reassuring hand on the arms of the people, though of course, their hands go right through the people's arms. Which makes the people even more upset.

Eventually all the ghosts go back to their tea sniffing and the people, who are alive, though very confused, stand in the middle of the teahouse, which is quite large, and loudly proclaim themselves as alive and "not supposed to be here."

Then, upon sniffing the wonderfully sniffiable tea that is being served to the ghosts, they begin to get a bit curious and find themselves sitting down at a tea table with some of the ghosts and to get interested in what kind of tea are they sniffing.

Upon learning that it is only the finest and impossibly expensive aged sheng puerh, they begin to get a bit excited and wonder if they may have a sniff, and possibly a taste of this wondrous brew.

Of course, the bodhisattva tea ghosts say, "*Mei wen ti*. No problem," and they bring out pots of this legendary tea from the 1930's, which the living people could never afford to buy and which they get visibly excited about.

When they are first served the tea, the living people first sniff the tea, just like the ghosts are doing, which makes many of the ghosts laugh. Then, the living ones begin to taste the tea, in small sips, of course, which makes some of the ghosts a bit jealous. If only we could taste the tea, they say, then we could really enjoy it to the fullest. But alas, they are ghosts and can only sniff the tea.

Chapter Fifteen

This tea is so magical and so amazing and so wonderful that the living ones begin to feel as though they might just want to stay here at the Teahouse For Ghosts, if they get to drink tea like this every day!

Its flavor is just so deep, and its qi is so rich, and its mouthfeel fills their mouth with a feeling of sweetness and bitterness both (like life itself) and seems to merge with their very own being, in a very substantial way, filling them with a feeling of goodness and joyousness. Sitting here, with their new ghost friends, and drinking this legendary tea, that was produced so long ago, gives them such a wonderful feeling!

Not only that, but as the living ones enjoy their tea, their new ghost friends start becoming a little less insubstantial and they, the living ones, start to feel lighter and brighter until it becomes a bit difficult to tell them apart. Then the so-called living and the so-called ghosts sit together in harmony, tasting and sniffing the marvelous tea and enjoying the marvelous moment together.

But eventually, the so-called living begin to appear more and more insubstantial and eventually they fade away entirely. Then they usually wake up in their own beds and lie there, wondering if it was all a dream or did they really travel to the Teahouse For Ghosts and get to drink that wondrous and outrageously expensive tea. Of course, it must be a dream, they think to themselves. After all, here I am alive in my bed and not in a Teahouse For Ghosts.

But then again, the flavor of that magical brew still seems to sit in their mouths, just a little, and they begin to look forward to dying, if only to be able to visit that marvelous teahouse again.

Chapter Sixteen

Happy Endings

Lulu loved happy endings, whether it was a book, a movie, a TV show or even on Facebook. Not that she had experienced too many happy endings in her own brief life. Her own life was a series of unfortunate events and even catastrophes. Orphaned at a young age, she was brought up as a ward of the state, living in a series of orphanages, each one bleaker and nastier than the one before it.

When she became of age, at eighteen years old, she was pushed out into the world, as if she were a piece of trash that no one wanted. And so, it often seemed to her, that she was indeed a piece of trash and did not deserve the love and emotional nourishment that she saw others receiving, just for being alive.

Yet she knew, deep in her lonely heart club band of one, that she did not deserve anything just for being alive. And so she tried her best to deserve what she wanted and needed, by being as cheerful and helpful and useful as she could be to everyone and anyone she came into contact with, friend or foe.

Not that she had many of the first. She was just so damnably cheerful and helpful in every single way that she creeped people out, and they turned away from her, even as she hoped they would turn towards her.

Lulu knew, from experience, that there was something deeply wrong with her, but what it was she could not understand nor express. She knew that her perpetual sunshine personality got on people's nerves and that it made them react with a deluge of dark clouds or worse, a full force gale of bad weather in her direction.

She had various jobs, all of them in the "service" industry—various fast-food joints where the service was dubious and the clientele often rude and obnoxious. She tried to be sparkly and welcoming to them all but, as time went on, she began to wilt in the face of the ugliness of the patrons, the atmosphere of too bright lights and too cheap ingredients, the piles of "pink sludge" that passed for food, the back breaking, long hours of work, and the greasy smell of her clothing and of herself that she carried home with her each night.

One blessed Sunday, she sat at her tiny kitchen table in her tiny kitchen and idly looked through the want ads, in hope of finding something that was not so heart and soul breaking. She sat and sipped her "instant" coffee and slowly read the many ads in the "service" industry until one suddenly leaped out at her.

Really, it was as if the small ad had actually leapt off the page at her, demanding her attention. "Wanted," it said, "server at small teahouse. Hours flexible. Apply in person." And the name of the teahouse was very strange. The Teahouse At The Edge Of The World, it said. Gosh, she thought to herself, I hope it isn't all the way on the other side of town. Lulu did not drive and so spent many long hours on buses trying to get from one part of town to another.

But when she looked at the address, it was quite near where she lived. Well, she thought, I don't really know much about tea, other than it comes in little bags. But the way her heart felt when the little ad leaped out at her made her think it was at least worth checking out.

So check it out she did. That very afternoon. She wasn't sure if it would be open on a Sunday but, "nothing ventured, nothing gained," she reminded herself. Though, in her case, it was usually, "everything ventured, nothing gained."

She went to the address listed in the ad but did not find any shop called, The Teahouse At The Edge Of The World. She crossed the street and went down the block on the other side but nothing there as well. Finally, before giving up completely, she went to the exact address listed in the ad and found a door with a small, even tiny sign that read, "Welcome to The Teahouse At The Edge Of The World."

She hesitated for a moment, then knocked as loud as she could. For a few minutes nothing happened, then the door slowly opened. It didn't creak like the doors in the scary movies she had watched at the orphanage, (the orphans there seemed to love scary movies, which Lulu did not love or even like), but it was a *little* scary, how slowly it opened.

Then a thin, white, even ghostly hand crept slowly out, followed by the smiling face of a very old woman. The lines in her face were more like gullies or ditches, no doubt worn into her face by much sadness and even suffering.

But her smile was very bright and looked much younger than the rest of her face. It was almost like a young person smiling behind the face of an old person!

"Hello," said Lulu, "I've come about the ad."

"Welcome, "said the woman. "Please come in." Then, she added, "You are most welcome here." And she said it in such a warm and friendly way that Lulu did feel very welcome indeed.

The door opened wider, and Lulu entered a very large room, with many small tables and chairs. It was completely empty of people, and she thought, it probably isn't open on Sundays.

The woman gestured to one of the tables and Lulu sat down, ready to begin describing her extensive resume' of "service jobs," (meaning soul sucking and heart-breaking ones), but the woman suddenly got up and went out of the room and through a door at the back of the room, undoubtedly the kitchen.

Lulu got a whiff from the kitchen as the woman went thru the door and immediately noticed that it did not have the usual greasy, depressing smell of the kitchens of her previous, unfortunate jobs. Instead, it smelled like flowers and dried grasses and something sweet and even happy. How could smells be happy? she asked herself. Yet happy it was, and even joyful, if that were possible (as it seemed it was).

Lulu sat at the small table, looking around the room. There were shelves and shelves of plants and tiny teapots and even what looked like round, flat cakes of tea. She couldn't imagine what kind of tea this could possibly be. Was it some kind of giant teabag?

Suddenly the young, old face of the woman popped up beside her. Lulu actually jumped, it was so sudden. "Oh, I am so sorry dear," said the woman, "I did not mean to startle you." Then she smiled her young woman in old woman smile and Lulu felt herself relaxing, as if all the troubles she constantly carried around with her, began to lighten a bit.

"My name is Meilin," said the woman.

That sounds like a Chinese name, thought Lulu.

"Oh," said Lulu, a bit flustered. "My name is Lulu."

"Lulu," said Meilin, slowly. "That almost sounds like a Chinese name."

Lulu wondered for a moment if the woman was reading her mind, repeating just what she had been thinking a moment earlier. But then she remembered that she did not believe in such things.

Meilin sat back in her chair and looked at Lulu for what seemed an endlessly long time. Then she nodded at her several times and for some reason, Lulu felt as she had just been judged and had passed the test.

"The tea that we serve here is very special tea," began Meilin. "Some people call it magical tea or healing tea or even heavenly tea. But really, all it is just very high quality tea." She looked over at Lulu and nodded again.

"We serve only Chinese tea," she said, "I hope that will not be a problem."

Lulu, who had been sitting there feeling a feeling of wanting very much to work at this wonderfully happy smelling teahouse, answered, "Oh no. I mean, I don't really know anything about Chinese tea but would be happy to learn. That is, if you are willing to teach me." She suddenly found she was holding her breath.

"Of course," said Meilin, enthusiastically. "I can see that you are a fast learner."

Which was odd, since Lulu had always felt and experienced herself as a very slow learner.

"When can you start?" asked Meilin, giving Lulu another of her young/old smiles.

"Any time," Lulu found herself saying.

"Great," said Meilin, "how about right away."

"Oh," said Lulu, "you mean like, tomorrow?"

"Oh no," said Meilin, "I mean like right now."

"Ok," said Lulu, who instead of feeling nervous about the whole thing, was finding herself feeling quite excited about the whole thing, which was very unlike her.

So Lulu spent that first day careening between joy and frustration and even fear. But over all, it seemed that joy was winning out. Of course, she felt completely out of her realm when the owner of the mysterious teahouse started teaching her about tea. She had never heard of tea being presented in that way. To her, tea was something that came in little bags, which you added milk and sugar to.

But here at The Teahouse At The Edge Of The World, tea was something altogether different and more magical, if such a word could be associated with something as mundane as tea. Actually as she would learn, tea was anything other but mundane, at least not the way it was presented in The Teahouse At The Edge Of The World. Here tea was

Chapter Sixteen

considered a medicine, a way to commune with the world of nature, which of course, is where tea itself came from. Funny, to Lulu, she always though of it as if it just came, fully formed, in the boxes of tea at the grocery store.

Not only that, but here tea was seen as a spiritual practice. Lulu had been raised as a Christian, but she had lost interest in it as she had grown up. She listened as the Meiling explained that tea itself was a gift from the Earth to the world of humans, from deep in Her heart. And it was when humans drank and shared that gift with others that the Earth communicated and even blessed them.

This was, of course, quite foreign to Lulu's way of looking at the world. She had never heard of such things as the Earth being alive and communicating with people! She thought about it all the way home after that first day at The Teahouse At The Edge Of The World. She thought about it when she fixed herself a simple supper and she thought about it the rest of the evening. Instead of sitting in front of the tv, as she usually did each evening, she made herself a cup of tea and thought about it some more. (Of course, the tea was cheap tea bag tea, but somehow she felt a feeling about it that was much different than before.)

She thought about it as she brushed her teeth and got ready for bed and she thought a lot more about as she lay in the dark of the night, before she dropped off into a deep sleep.

But just before dawn she had a dream, a tea dream. In the dream she was walking through a deep forest, filled with huge old trees. The trees were, of course, tea trees. (Meilin had told her that the most popular tea at The Teahouse At The Edge Of The World was puerh, which grew on trees, not bushes.)

The trees in her dream grew together in clusters, some of them even had their limbs (their arms) entwined. The limbs were also heavy with various kinds of mosses and looked very, very old. Meilin had told Lulu that some of them had roots going hundreds of feet into the Earth.

The living, breathing Earth.

Lulu walked through this cathedral of trees (which is how she saw and felt it), and let her hands trail through the low hanging limbs, her arms reaching out for theirs. She looked around and about and found that she felt safe, here in the ancient dense forest, safer than she had ever felt before.

Not only that, but she felt *accepted*, in a way that she had never felt around anyone in her short, sad life. It was as if the limbs of the trees were reaching out to her, as she reached out to them. As if they were in a sort of embrace, here in the deep, deep forest of living beings, of tea.

When she woke up she spent a little more time enjoying the dream. She couldn't wait to tell Meilin about it. Meilin, her new friend, and teacher and boss!

And sure enough, when she did tell Meilin she smiled a deep and lovely smile, her young smile in her old face. "Yes", she said, "tea is calling to you. She recognizes you. She knows you."

Lulu spent the rest of that day and for many days after, floating a little above the Earth—the living, breathing Earth—as she poured puerh for all the wonderful customers of The Teahouse At The Edge Of The World. She learned about all kinds of teas—green tea, black tea, red tea, and of course, puerh tea, the most magical one of them all. And she found that she did not have to try very hard to be recognized and accepted and welcomed by all the wonderful tea lovers that showed up each day.

As the days went on, she felt more and more at home there, in that cozy teahouse. She felt a sense of belonging that she had never felt before. At the end of the day, she felt happy, tired but happy, not drained and smelly like from her other jobs. And when she got home, instead of plopping herself in front of the tv, she brewed herself a small pot of very expensive tea. Of course, she got a discount from the teahouse and only bought very small batches of the most aged and wonderful tea in the world. Her world, at least.

She sat on her couch and looked out the window and watched as summer sprang into spring, and spring flowed into fall, and fall fell into winter, and then winter flew into summer again.

And, since she was still at the beginning of her journey, it was not the happy ending she had always dreamed of, but it was sure a happy beginning.

Epilogue

So here we have a few stories from The Teahouse At The Edge Of The World. I hope you have enjoyed them as much as I have collecting them from the far corners of the world and time.

I am sure there are many more floating around out there, like leaves of tea floating in a bowl or cup. Not only that, but there are more being created every day!

Every time a lost or wounded soul ventures out into the unknown; every time someone is exploring the wonder-filled world of tea; every time someone decides to believe in magic and miracles; every time someone lets go of who they think they have always been and instead opens up to becoming someone new and more—they may find themselves at The Teahouse At The Edge Of The World.

And who knows, someday you may find yourself at The Teahouse At The Edge Of The World and *your* story will become another story of this magical teahouse!

Solala Towler

About the Author

Solala Towler is author of 14 books on the Daoist arts. Solala teaches qigong, Daoist meditation and tea ceremony at workshops and conferences around the U.S., and leads tours to China and Taiwan to explore qigong, tea ceremony and Daoist meditation in the sacred mountains.

For more information on Solala's China trips, his books, and his workshops and classes, write to solala@abodetao.com or go to his website at www.abodetao.com.

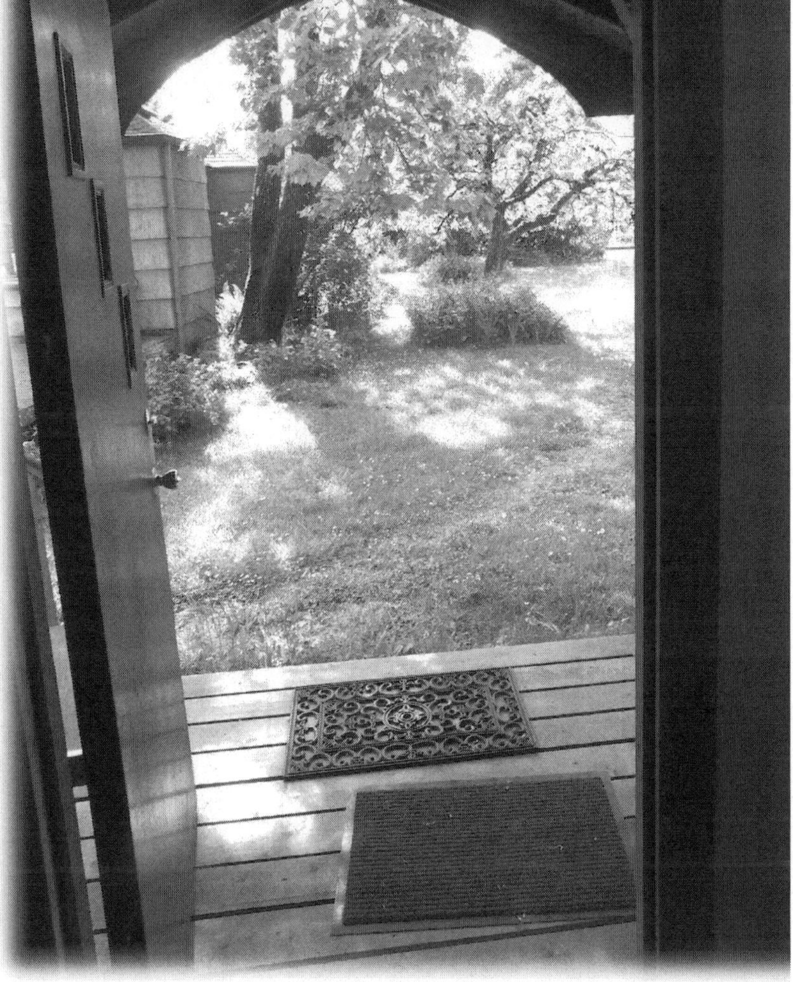

Made in the USA
Columbia, SC
24 February 2025